Aberdeenshire

Dear Reader,

I was so excited to get to have the opportunity to work on this series with so many other wonderful authors. I was especially excited to have a hero who was an FBI agent masquerading as a cowboy. What better combination could there be in a hero?

I just returned from a writer's retreat, where I enjoyed spending time with other writers and talking about ideas for new books. It was definitely two days of too much fun, lots of laughter and plenty of creativity flowing.

The weekend left me excited about new heroes and heroines and story ideas to hopefully keep you both on the edge of your seat and with a final sigh of happiness.

Hopefully in *Rancher Under Cover* you'll enjoy my red-haired heroine, Caitlin O'Donahue, who has a traumatic secret, and my hero, Rhett Kane, FBI agent working undercover as Randall Kane, a cowboy whose sole objective is to arrest Caitlin's father, an act he knows will destroy her. When their worlds collide, there will be danger, betrayal and secrets released that will forever change their lives.

Keep reading!

Carla Cassidy

RANCHER UNDER COVER

BY
CARLA CASSIDY

MILLS & BOON

First published in Great Britain 2012
by Mills & Boon, an imprint of Harlequin (UK) Limited,
Eton House, 18-24 Paradise Road, Richmond, Surrey TW9 1SR

Special thanks and acknowledgment to Carla Cassidy for her contribution to The Kelley Legacy miniseries.

© Harlequin Books S.A. 2011

ISBN: 978 0 263 89568 1
ebook ISBN: 978 1 408 97749 1

46-1012

Harlequin (UK) policy is to use papers that are natural, renewable and recyclable products and made from wood grown in sustainable forests. The logging and manufacturing processes conform to the legal environmental regulations of the country of origin.

Printed and bound in Spain
by Blackprint CPI, Barcelona

Carla Cassidy is an award-winning author who has written over eighty books for Mills & Boon. She won Best Silhouette Romance from *RT Book Reviews*. In 1998, she won a Career Achievement Award for Best Innovative Series from *RT Book Reviews*.

Carla believes the only thing better than curling up with a good book to read is sitting down at the computer with a good story to write. She's looking forward to writing many more books and bringing hours of pleasure to readers.

To Karen King,
who has taught me that friends can have philosophical
differences, intense debates on writing styles, and still
find joy and comfort in each other. Thanks for being a
good friend and seeing my flaws and liking me anyway!

Chapter 1

Caitlin O'Donahue nearly wept in relief as the O'Donahue ranch house came into view. The past two weeks
of her life had been the worst kind of nightmare, and
all that had kept her going, all that had kept her sane,
were thoughts of home.

The large two-story ranch house with its wraparound
porch and cheerful white trim instantly filled her with
a sense of safety, of security that had been absent from
her life over the course of the past couple of weeks.

*Coarse male laughter. Big rough hands holding her
wrists...her ankles. And pain. The kind of pain and fear
no woman should ever have to endure.*

She shook her head to banish the terrible memories.
She was safe now. She was home and the last thing

she wanted to do was dwell on the nightmare she'd so recently escaped.

She parked the car and got out, then walked to the trunk and pulled out her suitcase. Setting the case on the ground, she paused a moment to draw in a deep breath of the sweet California air and allowed her gaze to sweep over the pastures and rolling hills.

It was a beautiful November evening. Horses dotted a distant pasture, grazing peacefully and presenting a pastoral scene. There was a faint breeze and the sinking sun was coloring the western horizon. Caitlin drew in another breath as she continued to peruse the area.

That's when she saw him, a tall man standing just outside the barn door. Despite the distance she could tell his shoulders were broad beneath the white T-shirt, and his slim hips were encased in worn, tight jeans. His long, shaggy blond hair sparked in the fading autumn sunlight and she knew she'd never seen him before. If she had, she was sure she would have remembered.

It wasn't unusual for her not to know all the ranch hands that worked on the place. The turnover was huge and they came and went with a regularity she knew her father found frustrating.

Still, she could feel his piercing gaze on her as she carried her suitcase up the stairs to the front door. Of course, Caitlin was fairly accustomed to garnering male stares. You couldn't have her fiery red hair and an hourglass shape and not have men stare at you. It had never bothered her before, but now she found the male attention a bit upsetting.

She relaxed as she opened the door and stepped into the foyer. "Dad?" she yelled.

Esmeralda, the housekeeper, appeared and with a shriek of happiness hurried toward Caitlin and embraced her in a warm, tight hug.

Caitlin closed her eyes and relaxed even more as the scent of yeast and lavender surrounded her. It was the familiar scent of love. Caitlin's mother had died when she was three, and Esmeralda had been the mother figure in Caitlin's life.

She was finally released and Esmeralda stepped back, her black eyes filled with both love and concern. "I'm happy to see you but why are you home now? I thought you'd planned to be with the Doctors Without Borders program much longer."

"I got homesick." The lie fell smoothly off her lips. "Where's Dad?" As much as she adored Esmeralda, she was eager to see her father.

"Gone on business." Esmeralda linked arms with her. "What a pleasant surprise you are. I'm so happy to see you. The house has been far too quiet since your father left. Come into the kitchen where we can catch up."

They walked through the great room with its oversize leather couch and love seat, a stone fireplace that was rarely used and a wall full of electronic wonders that her father loved. The room smelled of the cigars he refused to give up and a slight lingering scent of his woodsy cologne.

She was bitterly disappointed that her father wasn't

home. She needed him not just for emotional support, but she also had some hard questions to ask him.

"Where did Dad go on business?" she asked when they'd reached the kitchen. She sat in a chair at the round oak table as Esmeralda went to the cabinet and took down two cups for tea.

"He didn't say." Esmeralda's plump features fell into a frown. "He left over a week ago and said he'd be in touch, but I haven't heard from him since then."

Tell your father his old friends say hello.

The words thundered in Caitlin's head, part of the memories she didn't want to revisit but that refused to leave her alone. What did it all mean? What had her father gotten himself involved in while she'd been out of the country?

Esmeralda put the teakettle on the stove burner and then carried the cups with tea bags to the table and sat across from Caitlin. "*Poco uno,* tell me what's happened. I see dark, unhappy shadows in your eyes."

Caitlin forced a laugh. "At thirty-four years old I'm not exactly a little one anymore, Esme."

"You will always be my *poco uno,*" Esmeralda replied firmly. "And I know my girl and something has happened to you. Talk to me, Caitlin."

A sudden thick emotion surged up inside Caitlin, but she shoved it away. She wasn't ready to talk of the horrors that had brought her home. It was all too fresh, too raw. "I'm just worried about Lana," she finally replied. "Has there been any word?"

Lana Kelley, Senator Hank Kelley's daughter, a close

friend of Caitlin's, had been kidnapped two months before. Caitlin had grown up with all the Kelley kids. She'd had a crush on the twins, Dylan and Cole, had treated the youngest boy, Jim, like a baby brother and had enjoyed Chase's company. She'd adored Jake before he'd left for a life in New York and had babysat for Lana. The babysitting had cemented a friendship between the two, a big sister/little sister relationship that Caitlin cherished.

The Kelleys had lived in California on a spread near the O'Donahue place for years, but as the years had gone by the children had grown up and sought their destinies away from the California mansion where their parents, Hank and Sarah, lived. While Hank split his time between Washington, D.C., and here. Lana had been the only one who had stayed at home.

Two weeks ago, in a brief phone call, Caitlin's father, Mickey, told Caitlin that Lana had been kidnapped while studying in Europe. He'd explained to her that the Kelleys weren't going to the authorities, but were negotiating with the kidnappers on their own.

"No news on Lana," Esme said, pulling Caitlin from her thoughts. "But there have now been six women who have come forward claiming to have been Hank's mistress."

"Six!" Caitlin shook her head, although she really wasn't surprised that the handsome senator had succumbed to what could only be considered a character flaw. There had certainly been plenty of politicians before him who had fallen to the same kind of demons.

Still, what a mess it had become for the entire Kelley family.

But she didn't care what consequences Hank faced for his infidelity. She was certain the handsome, powerful Senator would somehow survive his personal drama. What worried her was Lana.

The minute Caitlin had heard about Lana's kidnapping she'd contacted Cole Kelley to find out what was going on. What she'd learned had horrified her. According to him, Lana had been taken and nobody seemed to know what the kidnappers wanted or even if she was still alive.

"And according to the reports, one of those mistresses is pregnant and Hank has now disappeared from the public eye altogether. I don't know where he has gone," Esme said. "I quit paying attention to all the nonsense. But I think I heard he was at Cole's ranch in Montana."

"He's probably hiding out from his wife," Caitlin said drily. "She's got to be devastated by all this." Caitlin couldn't imagine that kind of betrayal by a man who was her husband.

"Caitlin, there is nothing that can be done about Hank and his problems, and we will pray for Lana's safe return." Esme jumped up as the teakettle began to whistle.

"You're right," Caitlin replied as Esme filled their cups with the hot water. "So, tell me what's happening around here." Caitlin definitely didn't want to think about Lana or Hank Kelley or anything but normal ranch gossip at the moment.

"That no-account Garrett Simms disappeared last week. Just didn't show up for work. He was nothing but a drunk anyway, but that left nobody in charge of the ranch, so I hired a new man." Esme looked sheepish. "I know it's really not my place, but your daddy was gone and this man showed up yesterday looking for work. He had good recommendations, so I told him we'd try him out."

"Is he tall with shaggy blond hair?" Caitlin thought of the man she'd seen when she'd first arrived.

"Blond and dimpled and absolutely divine," Esme said with an uncharacteristic girlish giggle.

"I hope he's as good with the livestock as he is at turning you into a giggling fool," Caitlin said drily.

"I think he's probably man enough to handle both jobs," Esme replied with a grin.

The very last thing Caitlin wanted to think about was any man. As she finished her tea and listened to Esme chatter about local gossip, she was struck by a weary exhaustion. She'd been traveling the better part of two days to get home and now all she wanted was the comfort of her room and a night of dreamless sleep.

"Do you want something to eat?" Esme asked as she carried their cups to the sink.

"No, I think I'll go upstairs, get unpacked and call it a night." Caitlin got up from the table and tried not to notice the ache of bruises that protested. Eventually they would heal, but she feared the scars inside her soul would be with her forever.

Minutes later she was inside her second-story bedroom. She should have moved out of her father's home long ago, but it had never really been an issue. Since her twenty-first birthday her father had always given her the freedom to come and go as she pleased.

She'd always enjoyed her father's company and knew he'd be lonely when she eventually decided to move. She'd respected him, a respect that had been recently shaken.

Tell your father his old friends say hello.

What had her father gotten himself mixed up in? And where was he now? She needed answers, but more than anything she'd needed his big strong arms around her, telling her she was going to be just fine.

It took her only minutes to unpack her suitcase and then she went into the adjoining bathroom and undressed for a quick shower.

Her father had raised her like a princess. She'd had the best that money could buy, the nicest clothing, the latest electronic toys, but she'd never cared about any of it. The best gift her father had given her was helping her fund the education that had led to her becoming a plastic surgeon.

Instead of opening her own practice she had opted to spend some time doing humanitarian work with the Doctors Without Borders organization.

She had loved the work, which had taken her to different places around the world. She'd felt as if she was making a real difference in the lives of the people she touched.

She had loved it until two weeks ago when she'd believed she was going to die in the jungles of El Salvador.

There was no question in her mind that she *would* have died if another doctor and several armed guards hadn't come looking for her. It was only as the band of men had been running away that the head honcho had said the words about her father. *Tell your father his old friends say hello.*

The hot water found each and every sore muscle she possessed. As she soaped her body she noticed the faint bruises that darkened her ribs. Thankfully they had almost disappeared, but the reason for them being there simmered inside her just beneath the surface, an agony she kept shoving away because she didn't want to deal with it.

Stepping out of the warm spray of water, she dried off and then pulled on a royal-blue silk nightgown. Outside the bedroom windows night had fallen. She moved to the window and stared out unseeing, her mind racing.

Where was Lana tonight? Lana, with her honey-blond hair and bright blue eyes. Was she even still alive? Caitlin didn't understand why the Kelleys hadn't gone to the authorities the minute Lana had been taken, but Mickey had told her that Hank was dealing with the situation in the best way to keep his beloved daughter alive. Caitlin made a note to herself to check in with Lana's brother Dylan the next day to find out the latest news.

She leaned her head against the cool glass of the window and released a sigh. Her best friend had been kidnapped and her friends the Kelleys were in trouble. Her own father was missing and she had no idea what his connection was to the men who had attacked her.

With a sense of foreboding, she turned away from the window. Suddenly, being home felt no safer than the jungles of El Salvador.

Rhett Kane watched the woman in the window, unable to help but notice how the dark-colored nightgown clung to her lush curves. The photos he'd seen of her hadn't done her justice.

That flaming-red long hair of hers would entice a man to tangle his fingers in it, to pull her head back to steal a kiss from her full lips. She had the body of a pinup—full breasts and hips and a tiny waist.

From the photos he'd seen of her he knew her face had beautiful, delicate features, that her eyes were gray and her lips plump without looking fake.

At least the intel he'd received that she was coming home from her work in Central America had been true. As her bedroom light went out he walked the short distance to the small corral near his foreman's cabin; a single horse stood in the center.

By the brilliant light of the full moon overhead he could see the emaciated condition of the young mare and the festering wounds on her flank that had been made by the rusty old barbed wire she'd tangled with at some point in time.

"Hey, girl," he said softly. The horse's ears flared back as she sidestepped, the whites of her eyes gleaming wildly in the moonlight that spilled down.

"You and I are going to become friends," he said. The horse backed up as if to protest his words.

Rhett remained at the corral for a few more minutes, sweet-talking the horse, who obviously wanted nothing to do with him. He finally left the corral and headed for his room in the nearby building. The horse needed wound care, but she was so stressed he worried she'd either kill herself or kill him if he tried to tend to her.

He was hoping to gentle her, to get her to trust him enough to allow him to take care of her, but that took time and he wasn't sure she—or he—had that kind of time.

All the other ranch hands lived off-site, which was fine with Rhett. He wasn't here for any male bonding. The last thing he needed was to make friends. His thoughts returned to the woman in the window.

Surely her presence here would work to his advantage. Mickey O'Donahue would get in touch with the daughter he loved, and if Rhett got close enough to Caitlin O'Donahue then he would be able to find out where the elder O'Donahue was hiding.

And he needed to find Mickey O'Donahue. Mickey had vital information that affected national security. It was crucial that he find him before other people did, people who wanted Mickey dead.

The cabin for the ranch foreman was located beside the stables and was small and furnished sparsely, holding a single bed and a chest of drawers. On top of the dresser was a microwave, and a mini refrigerator stood in one corner. The adjoining bathroom held a stool, a sink and a shower. Certainly not the lap of luxury, but it contained everything he needed, and besides, Rhett had been in much worse surroundings.

It took him only minutes to prepare for bed. He got comfortable, pulled up the sheet and fell asleep thinking about how best to use Caitlin O'Donahue to achieve his ultimate goal.

It was nine the next morning when he walked to the big house and knocked on the back door, eager to meet Caitlin in person. Esmeralda greeted him with a wide smile as she gestured him into the kitchen.

"Good morning, Mr. Kane," she said.

"Randall, I told you to call me Randall," he replied with a chiding grin.

Randall Kane existed for the sole purpose of finding the whereabouts of Mickey. The identity included a résumé of ranch work that would make him a desirable employee, a résumé that was surprisingly close to the life Rhett had led before tragedy had struck. Rhett knew the false identity and the résumé would stand up under normal scrutiny, and he was expecting nothing more than that in this case.

"Then it's Randall," Esmeralda agreed. She nodded and reached a hand up as if to check the tidiness of the dark, plump bun at the nape of her neck as her cheeks pinkened in pleasure. "Would you like a cup of coffee,

Randall? I just pulled homemade cinnamon rolls from the oven. Perhaps you'd like one of them?"

"They smell wonderful, but actually I was just wondering if you'd heard from the boss. I have something to discuss with him."

Her smile instantly fell and she shook her head. "No word from the boss, but his daughter, Caitlin, arrived last night. She should be down any minute and you can discuss whatever is necessary with her." She motioned him to the table. "Sit, and while you wait for her to come down you can have one of my rolls and a cup of fresh coffee."

Rhett slid into a chair at the table and watched as Esmeralda poured his coffee and then carried the cup and a saucer with a fat, iced cinnamon roll to him.

"I hope you slept well, Mr...Randall," she said as she sat in the chair opposite him.

He gave her a lazy wink. "When you work hard and live right you sleep like a baby every night."

She laughed, as if pleased by his words. He'd worked hard since arriving here to charm the older Hispanic woman, knowing that if for any reason Caitlin didn't show up at the ranch, the housekeeper might be his only path to finding Mickey O'Donahue's whereabouts.

He took a big bite of the cinnamon bun and rolled his eyes heavenward in pleasure. "Esmeralda, these are fit for the gods."

The plump housekeeper giggled and preened like a woman half her age. He finished the roll in two more bites.

"Good morning."

Esmeralda jumped out of her chair and Rhett turned to see Caitlin standing in the doorway. She was clad in a pair of tight jeans and a navy T-shirt that clung to her full breasts and emphasized her tiny waist, and her beauty momentarily stole his breath away.

Her glorious hair was pulled back at the nape of her neck, fully exposing the delicate bone structure of her face and emphasizing her gray eyes. He got up from his chair as she entered the kitchen.

"Caitlin, this is the man I told you about, the one I hired to take over for Garrett as foreman," Esmeralda said. "He's here to discuss some things with you."

"Randall Kane." He walked toward her and held out his hand with a smile.

She hesitated a beat and then gave his hand a quick, perfunctory shake. "Please, sit."

She smelled of something clean and lightly floral, a scent that instantly went to his head and kicked off a slight spark of warmth in the pit of his stomach. He returned to his chair and she slid into the one across from him that Esmeralda had vacated.

"I knew you'd be down as soon as you smelled these rolls," Esmeralda exclaimed as she poured Caitlin a cup of coffee and served her one of the hot treats. "My girl loves my cinnamon rolls."

Up close Rhett noticed that Caitlin's eyes weren't just an ordinary gray, but had indigo rings around the gray. They were beautiful eyes, but at the moment they gazed at him warily. "Where are you from, Mr. Kane?"

"I grew up in Wyoming," he replied. "And please, make it Randall. In recent years I'm from no place in particular. I go wherever I can find ranching work." He consciously willed away thoughts of the woman who had once been his home. The last thing he needed at the moment was to think about the wife he'd lost.

"Esme mentioned that you have references?"

He nodded. "I've got a résumé in my room. I'll bring it to you when I get a chance." He leaned forward and gave her his best charming grin, the one that he knew made the dimples dance in his whiskered cheeks. "Used to be all you needed to do for a ranching job was show up sober two days in a row. Nowadays everyone wants an official computer résumé."

"As far as I'm concerned computers are the devil's work," Esmeralda exclaimed. "And it's the same with cell phones and all the other electronic geegaws that suck the brains out of our youth."

Rhett laughed and then looked at Caitlin, surprised to see that she had paled to the point that the light smattering of freckles across the bridge of her nose appeared darker than they had moments before. "Are you okay?" he asked curiously.

"I'm fine." She wrapped her fingers around her coffee mug, as if seeking the warmth. "You needed to discuss something specifically with me?"

It was obvious she wanted him to state his business and then get out of her kitchen. "I don't know what your previous foreman did with his time, but it's obvious he wasn't paying attention to the health and welfare of your horses."

Her lovely eyes narrowed. "What are you talking about?"

"The horses are too lean, and yesterday afternoon I found one down in a bramble patch on the west side of the property. I don't know how long she'd been there, but she'd gotten tangled up in some old rusty barbed wire and she has a couple of festering wounds."

Caitlin's cheeks flared with color. "That good-for-nothing Garrett. I knew Dad should have fired him a long time ago. Where's the mare now?"

"I managed to get her up and into the small corral, but I haven't been able to tend to her wounds. She's scared and so thin I'm afraid the stress might kill her." A touch of anger lit up inside Rhett. Garrett Simms had obviously been a piss-poor foreman who hadn't regularly checked on the welfare of the livestock.

"Why don't I meet you at the stables in fifteen minutes," Caitlin said. "We'll ride the pasture and then I want to see that mare." She picked up her coffee cup and took a sip, her gaze going to the nearby window.

Rhett knew it was a dismissal and he got out of his chair and headed for the back door. "I'll see you out there," he said and then left the house.

As he walked back toward the small corral his thoughts raced with his impressions of Caitlin. Beautiful and sexy, there was no question about that, but she wasn't some bubble-headed woman riding on her outer appearance. There had been a keen intelligence shining from her amazing eyes.

What had shocked him more than anything was the swift kick of lust that had momentarily flared inside him when he'd been near her.

She'd certainly seemed unaffected by his attempt to charm her with his smile. In fact, she'd appeared reluctant even to touch his hand for a quick shake.

Her presence here could either be a gift from fate or a complication. He'd been intent on charming Esmeralda to get the information he needed in case Caitlin didn't show, but he knew the best way to find out about Mickey O'Donahue's whereabouts was through his daughter.

He'd use whatever means necessary to achieve his goal. He could be an accomplished liar and a pleasing lover if his role called for it.

Despite the fact that he'd felt a kick of desire for her, he didn't worry about getting his heart involved. He didn't have a heart to worry about. It had been trampled years ago and had never recovered from the wounds.

As far as he was concerned this was just another job and Caitlin was simply a hot, sexy mark to be used to get what he needed.

Chapter 2

Caitlin wasn't sure why she was reluctant to meet Randall outside. Although she was worried about the horses, the tall man with the shaggy blond hair and the five-o'clock shadow that darkened his firm jaw was too sexy, far too male for her comfort.

His brief laughter moments before had sounded nothing like the laughter of the men in the jungle, but for a moment sick memories had slammed into her and she'd felt an internal tremble.

She lingered over her coffee as Esme left the kitchen to attend to some household chores in another room. Caitlin felt fragile and weariness weighed heavily on her shoulders.

Terrible nightmares had plagued what little sleep

she'd gotten and she'd awakened feeling no more rested than she'd felt before going to bed the night before.

Glancing at the clock on the stove, she reluctantly got to her feet and carried her cup to the dishwasher. There was a part of her that didn't want to do anything but go back upstairs to her room and hide. Anxiety simmered inside her, threatening to explode into a full-blown panic attack.

She'd had enough psychology classes to recognize that what she was experiencing was normal for a woman who had been through what she'd endured. She suffered from more than a little bit of post-traumatic stress disorder. She understood the symptoms, but didn't feel as if she were in control of any of them.

She'd also learned in the past two weeks that the easiest way to cope with the emotions that churned just beneath the surface was to completely ignore them. She'd rather be numb than feel anything because she was terrified of what she might feel if she allowed herself.

With another glance at the clock she drew in a deep, steadying breath. She couldn't put it off any longer. She walked into the living room and to the ornate desk in the corner where a fat ceramic leprechaun smiled from his perch on the top. His stomach was hollow and stored paper clips, thumb tacks and the key to the gun cabinet.

She plucked out the key and moved to the large glass-enclosed cabinet and withdrew a revolver. After checking that it was loaded and the safety was on she tucked it into her jeans waistband and then returned the key to the leprechaun.

She knew how to handle a gun, was a good shot. Although her father often encouraged her to carry a gun when she was out riding the range because of wild critters like mountain lions and coyotes, Caitlin rarely did. She'd always figured any animals she might encounter would be more afraid of her than she was of them.

Today she wanted the weapon with her. She didn't know what kind of critter Randall Kane might be and she was determined never to be vulnerable again.

She stepped out the back door and into the warm November sunshine. The air smelled of earth and grass and horse, a familiar scent that momentarily filled her with a sense of home, of safety. However, the sense of safety vanished as she saw Randall Kane near the stables with two saddled horses.

You can do this, a little voice whispered inside her head. A ride around the pasture to check out the livestock didn't sound threatening in any way. Still, it would be the first time she'd been all alone with any man since the horrible event in the jungle.

As she approached him a lazy smile curved his lips and his hot, slightly scruffy handsomeness slammed into her chest with a force that surprised her.

She ignored the tightness in her chest and instead focused on the fact that one of the horses he'd saddled up was her favorite, Buttercup.

The horse greeted her with a soft whinny. "Hey, girl," she said as she stepped closer and rubbed Buttercup's nose.

"She looks happy to see you," Randall said. "One of the other hands told me she's the one you usually ride."

"She's definitely one of my favorites." She mounted the horse in a fluid motion that came from years of practice and then looked at Randall expectantly. "Let's ride."

He mounted his horse, Samson, with equal ease. "Are you expecting trouble?" Those gorgeous green eyes of his gazed pointedly at the gun she'd shoved in her waistband.

"No, just prepared for it if it comes," she replied and then with a flick of her reins headed toward the distant pastures.

He rode like a cowboy intimately familiar with the saddle, and she found herself wondering how he'd shown up at the O'Donahue ranch at such an opportune time.

Caitlin knew her father had been dissatisfied with the former foreman, Garrett Simms, for a long time, but had felt sorry for the alcoholic who played the victim card each time Mickey had tried to fire him.

But even Mickey wouldn't be able to overlook the abuse or neglect of any of his beloved horses, and there was no way Simms would be welcomed back this time. If nothing else she'd make sure of that.

She glanced at the man next to her and told herself not to look a gift horse in the mouth. Who knew why his timing was so perfect? The fact of the matter was, he was here and he seemed competent, and that would do until her father got home.

All thoughts of the man fled from her mind as the herd of horses came into view. Mickey O'Donahue had never wanted to raise champion race horses; rather he'd made part of his massive fortune raising good-natured saddle stock that was sold to individuals and various stables around the country.

The herd consisted of Tennessee walkers, mustangs and American quarter horses in a variety of colors and sizes. Caitlin pulled the reins to bring Buttercup to a halt and Randall reined in next to her.

"The pasture is a bit thin from lack of rain," he said. "What I'd like to do is add some oat hay into their diets until spring."

The horses did look lean…a little too lean. "Sounds reasonable," she agreed. "We work with Wilson's Feed Store. I'll call them when we get back to the house and place an order. They should be able to deliver it first thing in the morning."

He nodded and then pointed into the distance. "Over there by the fence is where I found the mare tangled up in the barbed wire."

She headed for the area with Randall close behind. Once again they came to a halt and she looked around with a frown. "I can't imagine how any barbed wire got here. Dad has never used it anywhere on the property." Despite the higher cost, solid wooden fences surrounded the pastures on the O'Donahue ranch. Mickey had never considered the cheaper alternative of barbed-wire fencing.

"It looked as if somebody had just driven by and

tossed it out of a truck or something," he replied. "After I got the horse loose I pulled it all out and took it to the dump."

She slid another glance his way, once again wondering where he'd come from and how he'd wound up here. "I'd like you to bring me that résumé we discussed earlier sometime this afternoon," she said.

"Not a problem," he replied agreeably. He shifted his weight in the saddle. "I understand you've been out of the country for a while."

"For a couple of months. I'm a plastic surgeon and was working in South America with Doctors Without Borders."

"Wow, must have been an amazing experience."

A sudden surge of emotion rose up in the back of her throat and she swallowed hard against it. *Amazing* wasn't exactly the adjective she'd use to describe her experience.

"I'm ready to see that mare now." She turned Buttercup around and as she headed back to the house she allowed the horse full rein. Buttercup responded by breaking into a run.

Caitlin hunkered low, the breeze in her face, the power of the animal beneath her easing some of the tension that had coiled tight inside her in the time since the attack.

She was vaguely conscious of her hair coming loose, flying wildly around her head as Buttercup raced like the wind. A sweet exhilaration filled her.

She'd needed this…the wild abandon that coursed

through her as she became one with the powerful horse. She gave herself to the moment, giving up any effort of control as she raced across the pasture.

All too quickly the small corral near the house came into view and she pulled on the reins to slow her gait, the moments of thoughtless pleasure now gone.

She pulled Buttercup to a halt and dismounted as Randall caught up with her. "That kind of riding is what I call chasing out the demons," he said as he dismounted, as well. His gaze slid the length of her, a lazy perusal that instantly jacked the tension back inside her. "So, Caitlin O'Donahue, exactly what demons were you exorcizing?"

There was a gleam of intelligence in his vivid green eyes and for some reason she felt as if he was attempting to peer into her soul.

It was a soul so shattered, so damaged that she wasn't sure she would ever let anyone in, especially not some hot cowboy she didn't know.

"No demons here," she replied as she broke eye contact with him. "I just enjoy the wind in my face." She tied up Buttercup and then looked at the mare in the corral.

The horse had run to the far corner of the enclosure when they'd shown up. Painfully thin, it was obvious she was both undernourished and frightened.

"Garrett Simms should be shot," she exclaimed, not hiding her disgust.

"My sentiments exactly. I have no idea how long she

was trapped in the wire, but from the look of her it was quite a while."

"Part of his job was riding the pasture to check on the health and well-being of the horses and it's obvious he wasn't doing his job. Good riddance is all I can say." She opened the gate and stepped into the corral with Randall following her.

The horse, a young mare she recognized, pawed the ground nervously as her ears went back flat. "Her name is Molly," Caitlin said. "Is she eating okay?"

"She's eating fine," he replied.

"You said she has some wounds on her?"

"On her backside," he replied. "I'd like to wash them out with some saline water and maybe get some anti-biotic cream on them. I was hoping she'd calm down, but I'm not sure that's going to happen and she really needs to be tended to. I can probably lasso her and maybe you could hold her head while I work on the wounds."

"That sounds like a plan," Caitlin agreed.

"I'll be right back."

Caitlin watched as Randall left the corral and headed for the nearby barn. He walked with a loose-hipped gait that screamed of sex appeal, and it surprised her that in her present state of mind she found him more than a little bit attractive.

She didn't want to go there, not with him, not with any man, not for a very long time. The very thought of a man touching her in any way filled her with a sicken-ing revulsion and made her realize just how wounded she'd been left.

It didn't take long for him to return with a length of rope, the saline solution and antibiotic cream, and a lightweight navy towel. He placed everything on the top of a fence post except the rope, which he gathered in his hands as he reentered the corral.

"This might take a few minutes," he said. "She's really frightened."

It was obvious Molly was scared to death. Her ears were pinned back and her tail was tucked between her legs as she backed away from Randall.

"Hey, baby girl," Randall said, his deep voice smooth and low. "Hey, Molly girl." He handled the rope as well as he'd ridden in the saddle.

As Molly sidestepped nervously and rolled her eyes, the terror the mare was obviously feeling resonated deep inside Caitlin.

Trapped.

The mare felt trapped, and Caitlin knew exactly how that felt. Caitlin's heart began to thunder with frantic beats as a shaking began deep inside her. Her throat narrowed, making her feel as if she were choking. Her chest ached as she tried to keep breathing.

Hands holding her down, men jeering and laughing at her terror. No way to fight back. No way to free herself from the danger.

She watched, frozen, as Randall cornered Molly against the back rails of the corral and tried to lasso her once…twice, both times without success.

Trapped.

The memories exploded again and again in her head,

hands holding her arms, her legs, making it impossible for her to move, to fight. *Help me,* a little voice cried in her head.

Leave her alone, she wanted to scream at Randall. *Can't you see she's terrified? Don't hurt her, just get away from her and let her go.*

"It's going to be all right. Everything is going to be just fine." Randall's soft voice broke through the memories that threatened to consume her.

Just breathe, she told herself, hoping to ward off the panic attack that was poised to spring. Thankfully, at that moment, Randall managed to lasso Molly around her neck.

"Grab that towel and the rest of the stuff," he shouted to her as he kept Molly's head tight against his chest.

Grateful for something to do, Caitlin quickly grabbed the items and hurried toward him. "Cover her eyes," he instructed and then began sweet-talking the horse once again.

The blindfold of the towel appeared to calm Molly somewhat. Although her body remained tensed, she didn't try to fight against him.

"Now, if you can hold her head, I'll take care of those wounds," he said.

Caitlin nodded and grabbed the rope from him. She held Molly's head close to her chest as Randall grabbed the saline and antibiotic cream and moved to the back of the horse.

"It's okay, girl. I know you're frightened, but the

worst is over now," Randall crooned to the horse. "You got through the scary part and now it's time to heal."

His words, coupled with the gentleness of his tone, seemed to reach inside Caitlin and drag a gentle finger over the ragged pain that knotted inside her.

A haunting vulnerability swept over her, as unwelcome as the agony that had been her companion over the past two weeks. She could listen to him forever, and the fact that his soft, soothing voice got to her also scared her.

He worked quickly and efficiently, Caitlin noted with relief, because she felt her composure slipping and needed to escape from Molly and, more importantly, from his soft, soothing voice that touched her, that somehow made her want to listen to him forever.

"That should do it," he said as he stepped away from the horse.

She let go of the rope, the need to escape from him overwhelming. "I have to get back to the house." She didn't wait for his response but ran out of the corral, determined not to break down where the hot, handsome cowboy might see her.

Rhett watched her go with narrowed eyes. There was something bubbling just beneath the surface of Caitlin O'Donahue. He'd seen it first when she'd taken off hell-bent for leather across the pasture.

Chasing out the demons. Although she'd said she just liked the wind in her face, he was sure that's what she'd been doing. And it begged the question, what kind of demons could possibly be lurking inside the lovely Caitlin?

He'd sensed a seethe of emotion coming from her again as she'd held Molly's rope. Tension had rolled off her in waves, a tension that was out of place with what was going on in the corral.

He was definitely intrigued, and it had been a long time since any woman had intrigued him. Of course it didn't hurt that the woman gave new meaning to the word *sexy*.

Still, when she'd taken off, riding fast and furious across the pasture, his heart had leaped into his throat as a sense of dreadful déjà vu shot panic through him.

He loosened Molly from the lasso and removed the towel from over her eyes. Instantly she danced away from him, wariness once again in her gaze, in her very stance.

He left the corral and his thoughts once again went back to that moment when Caitlin had dashed across the pasture. For a moment he'd been flung back in time, back to when he'd raced across a pasture with another woman, a woman who had tragically died in his arms.

That had been eight long years ago, when he'd been twenty-seven. At that time all he'd wanted in life was to work his ranch, love his wife, Rebecca, and have a couple of kids to add to his joy.

A wild ride across a pasture had destroyed it all, had nearly destroyed him. He glanced at the house and thought again of Caitlin. She intrigued him, and he definitely felt a kick of desire each time he saw her, but all he wanted here was to do his job, to get her father into custody.

The man had to show up sometime or at least let his daughter know where he was holed up. Rhett intended to get close enough to Caitlin to learn any information she might get about Mickey's whereabouts.

Rhett would do whatever it took to achieve his goal. He wasn't a happy, laid-back cowboy anymore. He'd spent years as a Detroit cop before being recruited by the FBI. As a federal agent he was doing his best to protect the President of the United States and he wasn't about to forget it.

The day passed quickly with chores that had to be done in order to maintain his undercover position as foreman of the ranch.

There were four other ranch hands and Rhett found them pleasant and competent men. They went about their business with little prodding from him and none of them seemed inclined to idle chitchat.

At noon the men all disappeared for lunch and Rhett headed for his cabin, where a microwavable pizza awaited him.

He'd just pulled it out of the refrigerator's tiny freezer when a knock fell on the door. He opened the door and looked at Caitlin in surprise. She appeared uncomfortable and held a covered plate in her hands. "Esmeralda made some extra fried chicken for lunch and thought you might like some. I figured I'd bring it out here and pick up that résumé you promised me."

Once again he noticed that she smelled of clean,

minty soap and some sort of exotic flowers, and the scent fired a tiny flame in the pit of his stomach. Her glorious hair was confined sedately at the nape of her neck instead of flowing free as it had done when she'd ridden Buttercup.

"I was just about to zap a pizza for lunch," he said as he took the plate from her. "I imagine Esmeralda's chicken is a much tastier choice."

He set the dish on the small table and noticed that she didn't cross the threshold into the room and that the gun she'd brought on the ride that morning was still stuck in her waistband. Interesting, he thought, that she felt she needed the weapon with her when delivering chicken to his doorstep.

"You want to join me?" he asked. "It looks like Esmeralda sent enough for five people."

"No, thanks, but if you could just get me your résumé I would appreciate it." She shifted from one foot to the other, obviously ill at ease.

"No problem." He went to the duffel bag on the floor and set it on the twin bed. "You make the business decisions around the ranch?" he asked as he rummaged in the bag.

"For now. At least until my father gets home."

"I would have thought he'd want to be here to welcome you back home. How long were you gone?" He pulled out one of the copies of the résumé that had been specifically prepared for him when he'd been assigned this job.

"A couple of months, but he didn't know I was

coming home." Tension was evident in her voice. She glanced back toward the house, as if wishing she were back inside and not on his little doorstep.

"Can't you call him on his cell phone or something?" Rhett handed her the résumé and then offered a charming smile. "I mean, I hate to get all settled in here and then find myself fired the minute your father comes home."

"Unfortunately he's not answering his cell phone and, in any case, if you do your job well then you don't have to worry about getting fired," she replied and took a step back from the door. "Thanks for this," she said as she held up the résumé. "If I have any questions about it I'll let you know."

Once again he found himself watching her as she walked away from him. She had a sensual sway to her hips that would naturally draw a man's eyes, but he still sensed a certain darkness in her...and a toughness. She definitely didn't seem to go all soft and gooey beneath the charm of his smile and dimples.

She probably had a boyfriend. He couldn't imagine a woman like her being alone, without any love interest in her life. A woman like her surely didn't want for male company.

Was she aware of what her father had gotten himself involved in? How much, if anything, did she knew about the secret society? She'd been out of the country for months. It was possible she knew nothing about anything that had come to light recently. It was also possible she knew and that was the stress he sensed in her.

Rhett was accustomed to women wanting to get close to him, finding him attractive, but Caitlin seemed to be the exception to the rule. She appeared as skittish and wary as Molly, but he was determined to get beneath her defenses.

She intrigued him, and she definitely kicked up a surprising dose of lust inside him, but that wouldn't stop him from manipulating her unmercifully to achieve his goals.

Micky O'Donahue stood at the window of the small motel room, watching as twilight began to fall. With the violet shadows of night beginning to edge in, a tense pressure built painfully inside his chest.

It was the same with the approach of each night since he'd left his ranch to go into hiding—the darkness brought with it a fear he'd never known before.

The darkness could hold danger and he'd never see it coming. Somebody could crash through the door, take him out with a single bullet to the heart.

He'd gotten in over his head, thrown his money and influence behind the wrong people, and now he didn't know what to do to get himself out of the mess, was afraid that he'd pay for his mistakes either with his life or with a life behind bars.

Hell, who was he kidding? Even if he wound up behind bars somebody from the society would find a way to get to him. He wouldn't last a week before somebody shanked him in the back or beat him to death.

He allowed the thick curtain to fall back across the

window and walked over to sit on the edge of the bed. Even if he wasn't scared senseless he'd find his surroundings horrifying.

The nightstand was scarred with cigarette burns and drink rings. The gold shag carpeting was certainly the original. The lumpy bed held no appeal and the water pressure in the bathroom was nearly nonexistent.

Mickey was accustomed to the best of everything and this seedy motel two hundred miles from his ranch was definitely depressing, but he also hoped it was the very last place on earth anyone would look for him.

He glanced at his cell phone on the nightstand and mentally cursed the fact that when he'd decided to take off and leave home he'd forgotten to pack the charger. The phone was dead. But maybe that was a good thing. He knew that with today's technology a cell phone registered in his name could lead searchers to him. Even if he had the charger he'd be afraid to use the phone.

Although he'd like to check in with Esmeralda, he was also afraid to call the landline at the ranch. It was probably bugged and there was no way he could chance somebody tracing the call and finding out that he was here. He needed to go out to get a disposable cell, but so far he'd been afraid to venture outside the room for anything.

Fear was a new emotion for Mickey. Sure, he'd been afraid when his wife had died and left him with a three-year-old to raise. He'd been scared then that he wouldn't measure up, wouldn't be the kind of father he wanted to be to his darling daughter.

But this kind of fear was something different, something completely new. It seeped into his bones with a sickening cold, tightened his gut until he thought he couldn't breathe.

He knew he couldn't stay here forever, that sooner or later he'd need to decide his next move. But the problem was, he didn't know who to trust. Mickey had always been a survivor. His craftiness and sense of self-preservation were what had made him successful in the political arena.

He'd been savvy, always with an eye to his own enrichment of power when it came to picking politicians to back. He'd only made one mistake—trusting Hank Kelley.

His stomach churned as he thought of the senator who had fallen from grace. Hank had been a good friend and a powerful ally over the years, but now he found himself embroiled in the same mess as Mickey. Even worse, Hank's daughter had been kidnapped by the very men Mickey feared were after him and now Hank was hiding out at his sons' ranch in Montana.

As Mickey thought of his own daughter his heart swelled with a combination of fierce love and pride. Caitlin was not only beautiful, she was smart. She'd breezed through medical school to become a plastic surgeon and he'd been proud of her decision to work with Doctors Without Borders before eventually opening her own practice.

There was only one thing Mickey loved more than power or money and that was his daughter. He hoped she would never know what her father had gotten involved in.

Once again he moved to the window to peer outside, the fear a rising lump in the back of his throat, a twisting coil in the pit of his stomach. The only thing that gave him any peace at all was the knowledge that Caitlin was safe and far away from all this, in South America doing charitable work.

Chapter 3

Caitlin stepped outside onto the front porch and breathed in the sweet scents of home. She sank onto one of the wicker chairs and settled in to watch the sunset.

She and her father often sat here together to enjoy the last gasp of day. They'd talk about the ranch, about the mother Caitlin couldn't remember and about life in general.

She'd always treasured that time to connect to the man who had been the best father a girl could ever want. They'd begun the ritual of watching the sunset together when she'd been a little girl.

If Hank was at the ranch, she wondered if Mickey was with him. What kind of trouble was her father in? As she remembered the words that had been said to her in the jungle, she was afraid that her father was in some sort of trouble with extremely dangerous men.

The fact that she now sat on the porch alone only added a final whimper to what had been a difficult day. Seeing how traumatized Molly was and then fighting off the panic attack that Randall's smooth voice had somehow produced had only been part of her stress.

She'd made a call to the Kelley ranch to find out if there was anything new on the missing Lana and had talked to Cole. What he'd told her had walked cold fingers up her spine. According to him, the men who had kidnapped Lana were now threatening to send snipers to kill all of the Kelley men.

Apparently Hank had sent a mercenary to try to rescue his daughter. The mercenary had been killed, but his action had infuriated the people who were holding Lana.

Caitlin had asked Cole why they hadn't gone to the authorities, but Cole told her there was a fear that doing so would instantly write Lana's death warrant. She'd pressed for more information, but Cole had been vague and then had ended the call.

There was also the issue of Caitlin's missing father. Even Esmeralda was concerned about the fact that there had been no word from Mickey. It wasn't like him just to disappear for any length of time and not stay in contact with the people at the ranch.

As if all of this wasn't enough to plague her mind, she'd found her gaze drifting from window to window throughout the afternoon to catch glimpses of the newest, very attractive ranch hand.

Randall Kane definitely threw her for a loop. She'd thought the traumatic event that had brought her home had also killed any emotion that any man might ever provoke in her, but she'd apparently been wrong.

Those men in the jungle hadn't killed everything inside her, although at the time she'd believed they had. Randall's bright green eyes, his strong jaw with those flashing dimples and his shaggy blond hair attracted her, and that was absolutely, positively shocking.

As if conjured up by her very thoughts alone, the object of her musings ambled into view. He was headed toward the foreman's quarters in the stable, but as he caught sight of her he changed directions and instead headed in her direction.

Instantly, a not entirely unpleasant tension twisted in her stomach. As he drew closer his sexy lips turned upward into a charming, lazy smile and he pulled the cowboy hat off his head.

"Beautiful evening," he said as he approached the porch. He didn't wait for an invitation from her but rather climbed the stairs, plopped down in the chair next to hers and placed his hat on the floor at his feet. "Wow, this is obviously the best seat in the state to watch the sun sink."

Caitlin nodded and told herself to relax as she gazed at the western sky that had begun to transform itself into an artist's palette of lush oranges, bright golds and vivid pinks. "I'm sure the sunset here is no more pretty than the ones at the Blackstone ranch in Wyoming."

He smiled. "Ah, so you had a chance to read my résumé."

"I not only read it, I called your last employer, Ralph Blackstone, who extolled your virtues and said you were nothing short of a miracle worker with horses."

"He's a nice man," he replied. "And he was a good and fair boss."

"It sounded like he was really sorry to see you go. What made you leave his ranch?" This was okay, she thought. She could still have an easy conversation with a man and not completely freak out.

He leaned back in the chair and stretched his long, lean legs out before him. "The wayward wind," he replied. Once again a smile lifted the corners of his mouth, a smile she felt in a small burst of warmth in her stomach. "The wind blows a certain way and I get restless and that's when I know it's time to move on."

"So, where's home?"

"No place anymore. As I told you before, I grew up on a ranch in Wyoming, but my parents died years ago, and with no family to tie me down, home is wherever the wind blows me."

"Most men your age have a wife and children," she said.

For just an instant his eyes darkened. "Not me. I'm built to travel light with nobody to take care of but myself. It's the way I want it, the way I like it." His eyes brightened. "What about you? You got some boyfriend lurking around the area?"

She shook her head. "No boyfriend."

"And why is that?" His gaze slid down the length of her, an assessing look that obviously pleased him and once again drizzled heat through her.

"I dated some in high school and then again in college, but when I got to medical school I just didn't have the time or the energy," she replied.

"You didn't find love in the jungle with one of those other doctors, huh?" His tone was light, half-teasing.

He sat close enough to her that she could smell him, a scent of leather and wind and a faint whisper of a sandalwood-based cologne.

There was nothing to remind her of the smell of the men in the jungle—that had been the odor of sweat and filth and the scent of her own fear. *Tell your father his old friends say hello.* The deep, malevolent voice exploded in her head.

"Hey, you okay?" Randall's deep voice banished the other one inside her head. She followed his gaze down to where her fingers clutched the ends of the armrests with white-knuckled intensity.

She consciously relaxed her grip and shifted positions in the chair. "I'm fine. I was just thinking for a minute about a friend of mine who is in trouble." It was a lie, but the minute she spoke the words thoughts of Lana jumped back in her mind.

"What kind of trouble?" His bright green eyes looked at her curiously.

Caitlin frowned, wondering how much she should tell him. Both her father and Cole Kelley had sworn her to secrecy where Lana's kidnapping was concerned, but she wished she could talk about everything to somebody.

"Bad trouble," she finally said. "But I really don't want to talk about it right now." Emotion rose up inside her and she consciously tamped it back. How had their lives gotten so screwed up? When would she get the answers she needed to understand what was happening?

"You sure you don't want to talk about it?"

She shook her head. "Definitely," she replied although it was a lie. She would have loved to talk about it, to tell somebody her fears, to have somebody tell her everything was going to be okay.

"Is there anything I can do?" His voice was soft and his green eyes glittered brightly in the failing light of day.

She looked at him in surprise. "Like what?"

His gaze continued to hold hers. "Oh, I don't know, maybe listen to you talk about it, or hold you if you feel like you need to cry or scream or something like that."

His offer was completely inappropriate but, surprisingly, there was a tiny part of her that wanted to be held in his strong arms while he told her, as he'd told Molly earlier that day, that the worst was over and she was going to be just fine.

"Thanks for the offer, but I'm used to taking care of myself." She was pleased that her voice remained calm and collected and held none of the wistfulness that had momentarily filled her.

"Still haven't heard from your father?"

"No, nothing," she replied, grateful for the change in topic, yet feeling a new tension ratcheting up inside her as she thought of her missing dad. "Maybe he'll be home by the weekend." It was Wednesday now and she could only hope that in the next couple of days he'd show up, contrite that he hadn't called to check in.

"Is this normal? For him just to take off and not let anyone know where he is?"

Once again she hesitated thoughtfully before replying and then decided giving Randall Kane some information wasn't a threat to her or her father. A cowboy who traveled whichever way the wind blew probably wouldn't be here long anyway.

"To be honest, this isn't in character for him and I can't imagine where he's gone or why he hasn't called," she confessed. "Although I'm assuming he thinks I'm still out of the country and that's why I haven't heard from him. I'm sure he'll be calling Esme soon to check in on things here and then he'll know that I'm home."

At least that's what she hoped. Even though she was a grown woman, she needed her dad here. He'd always made her feel safe and secure, had always made her feel protected and loved, and she needed to feel that more than ever right now.

She knew she should go inside, but Esme would already be in her private quarters at the back of the house and Caitlin knew the silence inside the house would be conducive to thinking, and that's exactly what she didn't want to do.

She looked at the handsome cowboy next to her once again. "Have you always been good with horses?"

"My mother used to joke that when I was young she'd check me occasionally to make sure I didn't have a horse's tail and mane because I'd rather be out in the barn with the horses than inside the house."

Caitlin was surprised to feel the smile that curved her lips at his story. It felt as if it had been years since she'd felt like smiling. "So, you grew up on a ranch."

"My father was a professional bull-rider and my mother was a barrel racer. Rodeos and horses were a way of life for us." He cast his gaze out to the distance where night had nearly fallen. "But it looks like your father has a thriving operation here."

"It is a thriving operation," she agreed. "But in the last couple of years this has become more of a hobby for dad than a passion. His real passion is politics."

"Really?" Randall sat up straighter in the chair and leaned toward her, as if finding it difficult to see her in the encroaching darkness. "Does he want to run for an office or something?"

"No, nothing like that. He much prefers to work behind the scenes. He's a money man, backing politicians he believes in and working the fundraising angles to get them elected."

"What kind of a man is he?"

Once again a smile curved Caitlin's lips as she thought of her dad. "He's bigger than life, although he's under six feet tall. His hair is a ginger color and he wears it long and pulled back in a ponytail. He's beefy and has had his nose broken more than once. He's a real man's man."

Randall's white teeth flashed in a grin. "You're telling me what he looks like but that doesn't tell me what kind of man I'm working for."

"He's a good man, loyal to a fault and with a great sense of humor. He likes good whiskey and expensive cigars and can break a horse that everyone else has deemed unbreakable. You'll find him a fair employer. Now I think it's time I call it a night." Her yearning for her father nearly overwhelmed her as she got up from the chair. He rose, as well. "Good night, Randall," she said.

As she moved toward the door there was an audible ping in the doorjamb. What was that? She froze in confusion and suddenly she was flat on her back on the floor of the porch with Randall's weight on top of her.

A scream lodged in the back of her throat. What was happening? Oh, God, what was he doing? Her brain shut down as sheer emotion exploded. The weight of him, the helplessness she felt beneath that weight shot her back in time, back to the jungle.

She could smell the rot of decaying vegetation mingling with the noxious odor of sour sweat. Hands held her legs, her wrists, making it impossible for her to escape as the men laughed at her.

Trapped! She was trapped and helpless.

Her heart screamed its beats in her chest as her throat

squeezed tight, refusing to emit a sound. Terror danced a macabre tango through her veins.

Someplace in the back of her mind she realized her wrists weren't being held, nor were her legs. She gasped a breath and released a pent-up scream.

She began to fight, just wanting the male weight off her, needing to get free before something terrible happened…something she'd already experienced and never wanted to experience again.

The bullet that had whacked into the woodwork of the door as they'd stood had caught Rhett completely off guard. But the last thing he'd expected when he'd tackled Caitlin to the floor to protect her was for her to turn into a scratching, fighting hellcat beneath him.

He fumbled and grabbed his gun from the ankle holster just inside his boot as he heard the distinctive thud of another bullet smacking nearby.

Dammit, what in the hell was going on? Who in the hell was shooting at them? As if the imminent danger of being shot wasn't enough, Caitlin struggled beneath him, trying to get free and making it impossible for him to focus on where the shooter might be hiding in the night.

"Caitlin, stop it," he hissed sharply. "Somebody is shooting at us. Dammit, stop fighting me. I'm trying to keep you safe. You have to stay down."

She froze and he thought he heard a small sob escape her. He raised his head just enough that he could look down at her, and in the faint spill of light coming from the front window saw that the indigo-blue ring around her pupils had expanded, nearly usurping the soft gray of her eyes. She somehow managed to look both confused and terrified at the same time.

"Listen carefully. I'm going to rise up and open the front door," he said softly. "When I do, I want you to crawl out from beneath me and get inside the door. Close it and lock it behind you and don't open it again until you hear me."

The confused expression on her face remained. "Caitlin, do you understand what I just said?" he asked with an edge of frustration.

"Yes, somebody shooting at us…crawl into the house and lock the door." Her voice was faint and half-breathless, but her eyes appeared more focused than they had a moment ago.

Rhett gripped his gun more tightly and eyed the doorknob nearby. His heart thundered in his chest as he stretched toward it and raised himself up. When he reached the knob he turned it and shoved open the door. "Go," he said urgently to Caitlin as he lifted himself up off her body.

She slithered out from beneath him and released what sounded like another sob as she crawled over the threshold. A second later the door slammed shut and he heard the lock fall into place.

Rhett breathed a sigh of relief but his relief was short-lived. He rolled to his side, facing outward and wondering where in the hell those bullets had come from. Darkness had fallen, making it impossible for him to see anyone in the immediate area. Whoever had fired those shots had apparently used a silencer for there had been no telltale explosion, only the whack of the bullets far too close.

He remained perfectly still, his head cocked as he listened for any sound that might tell him where the person was hiding, but all he could hear was the bang of his heart against his ribs.

His best hope was that the gunman would fire again and Rhett would see the flash of the shot in the darkness and be able to identify the location of the shooter.

Unfortunately, the only way he knew to make that happen was to rise up and make himself a target. Drawing in a deep, steadying breath he half rose to his feet, steeling himself for the potential of being shot.

Nothing happened. No flame of a gunshot, no thud of a bullet, nothing. He straightened and quickly jumped off the porch, then crouched low…waiting…watching. Still nothing happened.

There was no noise to indicate that there was anyone skulking around the area and night insects had begun their discordant songs once again.

He began to make his way across the yard, using tree trunks and whatever else he could find for cover. As he moved, his mind worked overtime.

Had the shooter somehow mistaken him for Mickey in the darkness of the night? It was the only scenario that made any real sense and it confirmed to him that Mickey was in deep. He obviously had information that somebody didn't want him to tell.

It was imperative that Rhett find the man before some of his cohorts did. Mickey's very life depended on it and they needed whatever information he might possess.

Was the friend in trouble that Caitlin had talked about really her father? What, if anything, did she know about the secret society and the mess her father was in?

After thirty minutes of searching the area, Rhett concluded that the shooter was gone. Perhaps he had recognized his mistake in thinking Rhett was Mickey and had stolen away in the night.

The stakes couldn't be higher and frustration rode Rhett's shoulders as he headed back to the house. Once there he knocked on the front door. "Caitlin, it's me. Open the door."

The lock clicked and the door eased open. She faced him, face void of color and a gun in her hand. "Point that thing someplace else. Remember, I'm a good guy," he said.

A red flush that matched her flaming hair filled her cheeks and she dropped her gun hand to her side. "Sorry, needless to say, I'm a bit on edge."

"Could you turn on the porch light?" he asked. She nodded and flipped a nearby switch. "Stay inside," he directed as he once again returned to the porch.

He found not two, but three places where bullets had struck. Three shots and any one of them could have connected. He ran his hand across the wounded wood, trying to discern which direction the bullets had come from.

He narrowed his gaze and stared into the distance,

figuring that the shooter must have hidden somewhere near the stables. Dammit, one of them could have been killed.

There was nothing more to do tonight and so he returned to the house where Caitlin awaited him, white-faced and nearly vibrating with tension.

"I'm assuming you didn't see anyone?" she asked as she motioned him to follow her into the living room.

"No, but I think maybe he was hiding near the stables."

She sank down into one of the easy chairs and placed her gun on the end table next to her. He sat on the edge of the sofa, adrenaline still coursing through him.

"You have any enemies?" he asked.

He wouldn't have thought it possible for her skin to go any paler, but it did. "Not that I'm aware of," she replied.

"What about your father?"

Her eyes widened slightly as a nerve pulsed in the side of her neck. "I can't imagine him having enemies that would try to shoot him as he sat on his front porch." She frowned and rubbed her forehead as her gaze slid to the left of him.

She was lying. He wasn't sure exactly what she knew, but she knew something about her father and he needed to find out what it was.

"Maybe I should ask if you have any enemies," she countered, her gaze once again locking with his. "I mean, this didn't happen before you showed up here."

He forced a dry laugh. "Not me. I don't stick around

long enough in one place to make enemies. We should probably call the police."

She shook her head vehemently, her flaming-red hair glistening in the artificial light overhead. Despite the circumstances, Rhett felt a crazy lick of lust warm his belly. His fingers itched to lose themselves in that glorious mane. Nothing like a brush with death to make a man want to make love with the nearest woman, he thought.

He tamped down his desire as he saw the fear that lurked in the depths of her eyes. "It's your call," he finally said.

"There's really no point in calling the authorities. We can't tell them anything that would help them catch whoever was out there. It would just be a waste of time to report this."

He had a feeling she was reluctant to call the authorities for another reason altogether—because she knew her father was in trouble and she didn't want to get the police involved. He wanted to ask her a hundred questions but knew now wasn't the time to push her. He couldn't overplay his hand or she would know that he wasn't just a good-old-boy wrangler.

She looked achingly vulnerable with that nerve ticking in her slender neck and her eyes dark and fathomless. Along with his desire to tangle his hands in that red hair of hers was also a crazy need to wrap her in his arms and pull her tight against him to assure her that he'd keep her safe from whatever she feared.

It was an unacceptable emotion, one that stunned

him and made him spring to his feet. "So, what do you plan to do about this?" he asked. "Of course, for all I know, the fact that somebody shot at us while we stood on your porch might be an everyday occurrence."

"Of course it isn't an everyday occurrence. I told you nothing like this has ever happened before, but I'm not sure what to do about it," she replied tersely. "All I know is that calling in a report would solve nothing and the only thing I can do from here on is stay aware." She picked up her gun from the end table. "I can take care of myself."

She might have wanted to appear strong and invincible with the gun in her hand, but he noticed that her full lower lip trembled ominously and her hand shook slightly. "I couldn't help but notice that you carry a gun," she said.

He nodded. "I don't go looking for trouble, but I'm always ready for it if it comes at me," he said, using almost the same words she had used when they'd taken their ride together and he'd mentioned her gun.

Her cheeks once again flushed with color. "I'm sorry I made it difficult for you by fighting when you were trying to keep me safe. I didn't know what was happening…what you were trying to do."

"I hope I didn't hurt you." He tried not to think about her warm body beneath his and the scent of her that had momentarily filled his head when he'd lain on top of her. "I just knew that standing up we were easy targets."

"Well, I appreciate it. I'd much rather have a couple

of splinters in my backside than a bullet through my head."

He gave her one of his legendary lazy grins. "If you need a little help picking some of those splinters out of your back I'd more than happy to offer my services."

"Thanks, but I'm fine, and on that note I think it's time for you to say good-night," she said as she placed her gun down and then rose from the chair.

She walked with him to the door and he turned back to look at her. "I don't know what happened here tonight, but I would definitely recommend that you keep your doors locked. I plan to sleep with one eye open."

For just a moment she looked achingly vulnerable with her shoulders slumped slightly forward and her eyes filled with shadows. A strand of her hair fell forward and before he realized his intention he reached out and tucked it behind her ear. Soft and silky, the feel of the curl seemed to imprint itself on his skin.

"Are you sure you're all right?" he asked softly.

Her lower lip trembled again and he wanted nothing more at that moment than to cover it with his own. He leaned toward her and she must have seen his intention in his eyes, for she quickly took a step back from him as her shoulders snapped rigid. "Good night, Randall."

"'Night," he replied and stepped out the door. His gaze swept the area at the same time he drew a deep lungful of the night air. He needed the fresh air to banish the desire Caitlin had evoked in him.

In all his years since the tragedy that had changed his life no woman had ever gotten under his skin, until now. And she was working her way under his skin by doing nothing more than appearing to be a strong, independent woman who, on second glance, had a wounded darkness in her eyes and a fragility that made him want to wrap her in his arms.

He had to keep his desire for her in check. As he left the porch his gaze continued to scan the area, but he sensed the threat was gone and he had a feeling Caitlin felt the same way.

Otherwise why hadn't she insisted they call the authorities? What woman in her right mind would be shot at on her own front porch and then dismiss the whole thing? It just didn't make sense.

He suspected that she believed what he did, that the shooter had been after Mickey and so she felt no further danger directed toward herself.

So, what did she know about all this? And more importantly how quickly could he get what he'd come here for so that he could escape from her haunted eyes, her lush lips and the emotions she stirred that held an edge of danger for him?

Chapter 4

Sleep had been next to impossible after the unsettling events of the night before. Caitlin finally got out of bed at nine the next morning, tormented by her own thoughts and the lingering aftermath of bad dreams.

Once she'd showered and dressed she had only one thought in her mind—to get some answers. There was no way she believed those bullets the night before had been intended for her or the new ranch foreman, and that meant they could only have been meant for her father.

She and her father had often sat on the front porch during the evenings. Although Randall was taller and leaner than Mickey, in the darkness of night she thought it would be relatively easy for the shooter to assume the man on the porch with her was her father.

So, why would somebody want to shoot Mickey? She

couldn't help but believe whatever trouble her father was in was tied to Hank Kelley, who had also dropped out of sight.

She'd hoped to get some answers from Hank's son Cole, but in the conversation she'd had with him he hadn't been forthcoming with any information that might explain either Lana's kidnapping or Mickey's disappearance.

She decided to call Dylan, Cole's twin brother, to see if he could give her more information than his brother had. She and the handsome Dylan had dated some years before when they'd both been teenagers. Their romantic relationship had fizzled after several dates, but through the years they had remained good friends.

Grabbing her cell phone she sat on the edge of her bed and dialed his number. Dylan was not only a high-powered lawyer, but she'd heard through the grapevine that he'd recently gotten romantically involved with Cindy Jensen, Hank's longtime aide.

She was happy for him if he'd found love. He was a good, solid man who deserved all the happiness that came his way.

"Dylan," she said when his deep voice answered. "It's me."

"Caitlin, how are you?"

"I'm fine, but I just got back into the country a couple of days ago and I need some information. I'm here at the ranch and Dad has disappeared, and with everything that's going on in your family I have a feeling he's involved in something bad. I need some answers, Dylan, and I'm hoping you'll give them to me."

"Caitlin, the less you know about all of this the better," he replied, his voice holding a deep weariness.

Caitlin bit back a sigh of frustration. "Last night somebody shot at my ranch foreman and I believe those bullets were meant for my father."

Tell your father his old friends say hello. She shook her head to dispel the voice. There was no way she intended to tell anyone about the trauma that had brought her home, and, in any case, one thing had nothing to do with the other. "Dylan, please. I need to know what my dad has gotten himself involved in."

There was a long moment of silence and then Dylan released a tired sigh. "I probably shouldn't tell you this, but somehow your father and mine got themselves involved in some sort of secret society called the Raven's Head Society."

Caitlin frowned and pressed the phone tighter against her ear. "A secret society? What kind of secret society?"

"One whose goal is to kill the President of the United States."

She gasped in horror. "That can't be true," she protested. "Both Hank and my father have supported President Colton through the years. My dad could never be involved in something that terrible."

Joe Colton was a popular president, known for promoting peace and fighting corruption. There was no question he'd stepped on some toes, made some enemies in achieving his altruistic goals, but there was no way

Caitlin would believe her father had become one of his enemies.

"According to my father, they didn't know what they were getting involved in. The Raven's Head Society was just supposed to be a group of wealthy businessmen and politicians working together to get the country back on its feet after the financial fallout of the last couple of years. It wasn't until your father and mine were in too deep that they realized the true goal and tried to get out."

Caitlin's head reeled with the information. A secret society? The death of a president? It couldn't be true. How on earth had her father managed to get himself involved in something so terrible?

"Where's your father, Dylan?" she asked. "I heard he's disappeared from sight, that he's at the ranch. Is my father with him?"

"Dad is there, but I can tell you for sure that Mickey isn't with him," Dylan replied.

"Why doesn't your father just tell everything he knows to the FBI or the CIA or whatever?"

"Because members from the society have Lana."

Caitlin's heart chilled at his words. Now she understood better what had kept the Kelleys silent. "So what do they want?"

"They want my father to take the fall for the rest of the society and then commit suicide in order to protect the rest of the members." Dylan's voice trembled slightly with what sounded like suppressed emotion.

Caitlin knew Hank had never been close to any of

his sons, and the reports of Hank's womanizing must have deepened the breach, but there was no doubt that Dylan was worried about both his sister and his father.

Dylan cleared his throat and continued. "We're trying to figure out a way to get Lana back safe and sound and keep Dad alive. Dad has been in touch with the kidnappers and has demanded proof of life where Lana is concerned."

Proof of life. The very words sounded so ominous and the implication of needing such a thing was horrifying. Her heart crunched as she thought of her friend. Beautiful Lana with her sweet innocence—she was not only gorgeous but was also an accomplished artist and studying to get her master's degree in art history.

Was she already dead? The question ached in Caitlin's heart. She couldn't imagine life without the woman she considered her little sister.

"Caitlin, wherever your father is, there's no question that he's in danger. There are members of the society who wouldn't blink twice before killing him. They consider him a threat to everything they want. If he contacts you, encourage him to turn himself in. Maybe he'll listen to reason better than my father is doing at the moment."

Caitlin thanked Dylan for being up front with her, and when the call ended she remained on the bed, overwhelmed by the information she'd received.

How on earth had Hank and her father gotten themselves into such a mess? Even as the question formed in her mind the answer came to her: they were both power-seekers and their hunt for power and influence had landed them in a dangerous mess.

She was smart enough to know that if Mickey turned himself in, he would probably be facing prison time for his involvement in any plot to kill the President of the United States. She also knew her father well enough to know that he'd rather be dead than live out the rest of his life in any prison.

Certainly this information made it more than likely that the attack last night had to do with somebody trying to kill her father. She wanted him home, but she also wanted him safe.

Tell your father his old friends say hello.

The voice exploded in her head, bringing with it memories that ripped at her soul, tore through her head. Had the men in the jungle somehow been a part of the secret society? Had that been a warning to her father? It seemed impossible to believe. The jungle of El Salvador was a world away from the political machinations of Washington, D.C.

Thick emotion rose up in the back of her throat and squeezed her lungs. The odor of jungle rot filled her head and she jumped up off the bed and mentally shoved back against the memories.

Dead. She needed to be emotionally dead in order to put one foot in front of the other, in order to face herself in the mirror.

The Kelley family was in crisis, but so were she and her father. She walked to the window and peered out.

Where are you, Dad? I need you here with me. I need you to help me understand.

There was nothing she could do until her dad surfaced. She hoped he'd call the ranch, check in, and then she could talk to him, tell him she needed him and wanted him home.

Once he was back at the ranch they could figure out his next move. As far as she was concerned he needed to go to the authorities and tell them whatever he could about the Raven's Head Society. It was the right thing to do and Mickey had always encouraged her to do the right thing. Surely he could be put in some sort of protective custody to make sure he remained safe.

Needing some fresh air, she headed downstairs and was greeted by Esme in the kitchen. "Ah, I thought maybe you were going to sleep the day away," the housekeeper said.

"I was just on the phone with Dylan, trying to find out if he or any of the Kelleys have any idea where Dad might be," Caitlin replied.

"Did he know?" Esme asked, a dark worry filling her eyes.

"No." There was no way Caitlin intended to tell Esme everything she'd learned from Dylan. She knew Esme's penchant for making herself sick when she worried. "I just wish he'd call and let us know he's okay."

"This just isn't like him," Esme said more to herself than to Caitlin. "Are you ready for some breakfast?" As always Esme figured food could fix any problem. "I baked some blueberry muffins this morning."

"Maybe later. I'm going to head out and check on a horse." What Caitlin wanted more than anything at the moment was a distraction from her own thoughts, her own feelings. Besides, there was nothing she could do about her father until he got in contact with her.

She stepped outside and, although the warmth of the morning air attempted to heat the chill inside her, it didn't work. Dylan's words had created a cold spot inside her very soul that she wasn't sure would ever be warm again.

It was only when she spied Randall near the small corral that a flutter of heat fired through her. He had a saddle draped over a sawhorse and was polishing the leather.

He didn't see her and for a moment she stood perfectly still and gazed at him. As he worked on the saddle his biceps tightened and his shoulders seemed to expand with his efforts. Definitely hunk material.

She'd thought he was going to kiss her the night before. There had been a moment when he'd tucked her hair behind her ear and she'd been certain that a kiss was his intention.

And what would have happened if she'd allowed him to kiss her? Would his closeness to her yank her back into the not-so-distant past? Would the feel of his lips against hers, the weight of his arms around her thrust her into a horrifying, embarrassing panic attack?

Right now she couldn't imagine being intimate with a man ever again. The thought of a man's weight on top of her, of grasping hands and hot breath caused a wild panic to attempt to possess her.

At that moment Randall looked up and the sexy smile that curved his lips at the sight of her shot another small burst of heat through her and tamped down the rising sense of panic that had momentarily gripped her. "Good morning," he said.

His shaggy blond hair gleamed in the sunlight overhead and his eyes appeared even greener in the light of day. Whiskers darkened his jaw, only adding to his bad-boy attractiveness.

"Good morning to you," she replied. "I just thought I'd come out and check on Molly."

The horse stood at the back of the corral, watching them with a wariness that broke Caitlin's heart. Whether it was something Garrett Simms had done to her or the time she'd spent wrapped up in that barbed wire, Molly was obviously traumatized. Caitlin could definitely relate.

Randall set the rag he'd been using to polish the leather on the edge of the sawhorse and straightened. "From what I can tell, her wounds look a little better today, but mentally she still seems to be in a bad place. I decided to do a little work out here where she could see me and maybe learn to trust again."

Caitlin leaned against the fence a small distance from him, although from where she stood she could smell the scent of his minty soap mingling with the saddle leather. It was a pleasant scent that could go to her head if she allowed it.

"I've been trying to entice her with some bits of apple," he said and pointed to several apple slices on top of the fence post. He picked up a piece and walked to the gate and entered the corral.

As he approached the horse Caitlin couldn't help but notice the broadness of his shoulders, the slim hips that wore the tight jeans as if they'd been specifically tailored just for him. His boots were dusty and worn, as cowboy boots should be, and he walked with the confidence of a man who knew his place in life.

"Hey, sweet girl," he crooned in that sexy deep voice that stirred Caitlin on a level that both made her uncomfortable and yet pulled out a crazy yearning inside her. "Hi, Molly."

Molly backed up, ears back and nostrils flared as Randall approached. Once again Caitlin felt the mare's fear resonating through her. But Randall's soft, soothing voice calmed the rising panic inside her.

He stopped when he was about four feet from the horse and held out the piece of apple. Molly pawed the ground and backed up until she could go no farther, obviously wanting nothing to do with him or the fruity treat he offered.

"I don't know what you've suffered, but it's okay now." He continued to sweet-talk the horse and, just like the day before, Caitlin found his deep voice, the words he used, a strange balm to her own broken spirit.

Still, it was obvious Molly wasn't going to let go of her fear, and he finally threw the apple slice on the ground near her and then backed away. Molly watched him until he'd exited the corral again and closed the gate, and only then did she lower her head to the apple.

"It's going to take some time," he said as he returned to Caitlin's side, standing far too close to her for her comfort. "She wants to trust, but she's still too afraid."

Caitlin moved a couple of inches from him and released a sigh. "She's a sweet horse. I hate to see her in this sad state of mind." Would *she* ever learn to trust again? Caitlin wondered if she'd ever trust as she had before El Salvador.

He turned to look at her. "Speaking of state of mind, how are you doing this morning? Have you figured out what that was all about last night?"

Yes, my father has gotten involved with a secret society that wants to assassinate the President of the United States, and I think it was members of that society that shot at you last night because they thought you were my father and they want to permanently silence him.

"No, I don't have a clue," she replied. How could she tell this virtual stranger what was going on? There was nothing he could do about it, and it was private family business. God, she so needed to speak to her father, to have him explain.

"The oat hay was delivered this morning. I put a couple of bales out in the pasture for the herd and the rest is stored in the barn."

"Good," Caitlin replied. "I hope that will make a difference."

For a long moment neither of them spoke. Caitlin focused on Molly, but was aware of Randall's gaze lingering on her. "Why plastic surgery?" he asked. "I'm assuming it wasn't just to keep you looking as beautiful over time as you look right now."

Once again she felt as if he'd somehow stepped over the boundaries of employer/employee, but when she shot her gaze to his it was impossible to be offended.

His incredible green eyes held nothing but open curiosity and she reminded herself that he couldn't know that being told she was beautiful was something she didn't want right now.

"Actually, I knew I wanted to be a plastic surgeon when I was nine years old and met Annie Fortner."

"And who was Annie Fortner?"

"She was a very bright fourth-grader who came to my private school on an academic scholarship." Caitlin began to relax as she remembered the dark-haired, dark-eyed girl who had been in her class. "She was painfully shy and withdrawn because she had been born with a cleft palate."

"That's tough," Randall said.

She nodded. "Some of the kids made fun of her and one day she told me that her parents were saving up the money to take her to a plastic surgeon to have it fixed. Apparently they hadn't been able to afford it. But the next year she came back to school and during the summer the plastic surgeon had worked wonders. Annie was like a different girl, filled with happiness and a real chatterbox. I knew then that when I grew up I wanted to be a plastic surgeon and make a difference for people like Annie."

"Nice," he said simply but there was a light of respect in his eyes. "It would have been easy for you to head to Beverly Hills and set up a practice injecting bored, wealthy housewives with pig fat or goat belly or whatever it is they use to plump their cheeks and lips."

She laughed, the expression of amusement not only shocking her but warming her, as well. "I do intend to eventually open up my own practice, but there will be no pig fat or goat belly in any of my work," she exclaimed.

"Well, that's good to know." He grinned at her and for a moment she felt a crazy connection to him. *It's nothing more than the connection of shared laughter,* she told herself. Laughter that had momentarily made her forget everything that had her worried.

In any case it could be nothing more than that. He might think she was beautiful. He might want to kiss her and even take it further, but she was unavailable, both emotionally and physically.

It had nothing to do with the fact that he was a transient ranch hand and probably wouldn't stick around for long. Nor was it because she had no idea what kind of trouble her father was in.

Rather it had to do with the knowledge that the jungle had forever changed her. She'd once dreamed of a special man, of passionate love and perhaps a couple of children, but those dreams had been ripped away from her.

Even though she found herself experiencing a strange draw to Randall, nothing would ever come from it.

The jungle had destroyed her. Randall Kane might

not know it but no matter how his much his deep, sexy voice called to her, no matter how much heat his gaze held when he looked at her, she was a dead woman walking, and to pretend otherwise would be a mistake.

Marc Jiminez sat on the sofa in his jungle compound and muttered a curse beneath his breath as he waited for the news he hoped to hear. His cell phone sat next to him and he willed it to ring with Juan Gonzales telling him that he'd accomplished what he'd been sent to the United States to do.

Marc had no toleration for failure. If Juan couldn't do what needed to be done, then Marc would send somebody else to take care of the problem and dispose of Juan at the same time.

No loose ends. That's what had kept Marc safe and successful for so long. Never give a witness a chance to talk. It was a creed that had served him well over the years.

Now it was time for Marc to make the biggest move of his life and there was only one thing holding him back from success—Caitlin O'Donahue.

He'd been following instructions from his contact in the Raven's Head Society when he and his men had dragged her off from her encampment and into the jungle for the sole purpose of warning her father that he and his loved ones weren't out of their reach. It was to serve as a warning that if Mickey decided to go to the authorities with what he knew about the organization, then neither he nor his daughter would survive the wrath of the society.

He'd been told only to scare her. The rape had been his idea. When he'd seen her struggling against the men who held her, her powerlessness, the terror in her huge eyes had sparked a darkness in him that he hadn't known he possessed, and he'd been unable to resist.

The minute he was finished he knew he'd have to kill her, but unfortunately before that could happen one of the other doctors from her camp, along with several armed guards, had approached and Marc and his men had disappeared back into the jungle.

Now she was a liability to his plans for taking his place in the United States, for being a respectable businessman with the power and influence of the Raven's Head Society behind him.

He leaned his head back and closed his eyes, imagining taking the position he'd been born to take back in the States. He'd been born in Washington, D.C., but then his missionary parents had moved to Central America to do their charitable work.

By the time he was twenty-two his parents were dead and he'd become one of the youngest and most powerful drug lords in the country. He'd quickly gained a reputation for being utterly ruthless. He'd clawed and killed his way to the top, always with the knowledge that one day he would return to his own country and leave this jungle behind.

Now he was ready to leave and begin a new life in the States. Here, he was surrounded by armed guards whose job it was to keep him alive. Here, men looked at him in fear but without any real respect.

Things would be different when he left this world behind. He would be a business man and men would look at him with respect. They would want him in their social circles and he would know the taste of real power.

The sky was the limit for him when he began his new life, but first he had to make sure that the woman who could identify him as a drug lord, the woman who could testify against him in a rape trial and ruin everything was dead.

Anticipation sang through him as his phone rang. "Is it done?" he asked.

There was a long hesitation. "Not yet," Juan replied. "I need a little more time. She only just arrived at her family's ranch."

Irritation swept through Marc. "How much more time?"

"I don't know." There was a hint of a whine in Juan's voice. "I need to wait until she ventures out of the house alone. She hasn't really left the place since she arrived and she'd been with one of the ranch hands when she's been outside."

"You have a week," Marc replied. "Find a way to get it done, Juan, or I'll find somebody who can take care of all my loose ends."

"It will be done," Juan replied.

Marc hung up and couldn't help the smile that curved his lips. All the work he'd accomplished through his life, his connections with the Raven's Head Society and now the death of Caitlin O'Donahue would assure a successful transition from the jungle into high society in the States.

Chapter 5

For the tenth time in the past hour Rhett's gaze shot
to the house in hopes of seeing Caitlin walking out the
door. He'd finished up the morning chores long ago,
including checking out the area around the stables for
any sign of the shooter. He'd found nothing, but then,
he hadn't really expected to.

Whoever had fired those shots had been careful not
to be seen, had used a silencer. Certainly that meant
the shooter had been professional enough not to make
a silly mistake and leave some sort of evidence behind
that could be used to identify him.

Rhett now leaned on the top rail of the small corral
that enclosed Molly. It was lunchtime, but before going
in he'd wanted to check on the mare.

As much as he'd like to spend all his spare time

trying to gentle Molly, he knew part of his reason for lingering here was in hopes that Caitlin would join him.

He'd enjoyed their brief conversation here the day before. He liked what he saw when he looked at Caitlin O'Donahue, but more importantly he liked who she was—a beautiful, sexy woman who was both smart and compassionate.

She fascinated him in that he sensed a bit of darkness inside her and he wasn't sure if it was because of the mess her father had gotten himself in or something else altogether.

But he was intrigued enough to want to find out. It was his job to find out, to get close enough for her to confide in him, he reminded himself for the hundredth time.

Of course, he was well aware of the fact that no matter how close he got to her, no matter how much he gained her trust now, she'd hate him when this was all over.

There was no question that she was tight with her father, that Mickey O'Donahue was something of a hero in his daughter's eyes. He'd raised her single-handedly, a fact that had certainly deepened the father/daughter bond.

The minute Rhett identified himself as an FBI agent and placed Mickey under arrest, he knew Caitlin would be devastated. She'd feel betrayed on the deepest level. She would be considered collateral damage that couldn't be helped, and he was surprised to realize he felt bad about it.

But this case was too big, the stakes far too high to worry about a daughter's emotional state. Still, before he could break her trust he had to gain it, and he wasn't there yet, not by a long shot.

There was a wariness that darkened her eyes if he stepped too close to her, a flash of wild panic when he touched her in the most simple way. Rhett wasn't used to women reacting to him that way. He knew he'd been blessed with good looks. He wasn't necessarily conceited about it, but was aware that his physical attractiveness drew women easily. Usually women seemed to enjoy his touch rather than avoid it.

In the best of worlds, he'd have time to woo her gently, to slowly build a relationship that would inspire her to trust and confide in him. But he didn't have time to move slowly. With the life of the president hanging in the balance, time was of the essence.

Checking his watch, he decided to head in for lunch. He zapped a Salisbury-steak TV dinner, and as he ate, his thoughts continued to be consumed by Caitlin.

In checking out Mickey, the information they'd gathered was that his daughter would be out of the country for a year, but then she'd suddenly decided to return home. Definitely a bonus for him, but what had brought her home earlier than expected? Had it been the knowledge that her father was in trouble or something else?

He finished eating, washed up the silverware in the sink and headed back outside. He opened the door and nearly walked into Caitlin.

"Whoa," he exclaimed as his hands grabbed her

shoulders to steady her. "I didn't mean to practically run you over."

"It's all right." She quickly backed away from him.

His arms reluctantly dropped to his sides. She looked stunning with her hair sparkling in the sunshine, clad in a pair of tight jeans and a royal-blue T-shirt that made the indigo ring around her eyes more prominent. At least he didn't see the gun shoved in her waistband, definitely a step in the right direction.

"What's up?" he asked as he tried to ignore the sizzle in the pit of his stomach at the very sight of her.

"Esme is making her famous tacos for dinner tonight and she wondered if you'd want to join us for the meal. She knows the cooking is limited out here."

"That's very nice of her," he replied. "And what does Caitlin want? Would she like me to join her for the evening meal?"

A tight smile whispered across her features and then quickly disappeared. "I'd enjoy a little company."

"Then I'd love to come to dinner. What time should I be there?"

"Around six?"

"Sounds perfect."

"I'll see you then," he replied, unsurprised when she quickly nodded and then turned and left. What did surprise him was the invitation, definitely a pleasant surprise, and the opportunity to dig a little deeper to find out what information she might have concerning her father and his whereabouts.

Although she professed not to know where he was,

Rhett wasn't sure he believed her. There was no question in his mind that she was a woman with secrets—and he was determined to learn all of them.

He didn't see her again for the rest of the afternoon and at five he finally knocked off working to head back in and shower. As he stood beneath the warm spray of water he wasn't sure whether the anticipation he felt flooding through him was due more to the possibility of getting answers or because something about Caitlin excited him as a man.

It had been eight years since he'd lost Rebecca and in those years there had been a few other women, but they'd been nothing but fleeting, temporary relationships with his heart not involved. None of those women had touched him on an emotional level the way Caitlin threatened to do.

Maybe it was because she reminded him of the woman he'd loved with all his heart and soul, the woman who had been stolen away from him by a cruel fate.

Certainly Caitlin didn't look like Rebecca, who had been a cool blonde with chocolate-colored eyes, but there were definitely similarities between the two.

Rebecca had been a charitable woman, always involved in giving back to the community where they'd lived and going to school to be a social worker. It was obvious from the choices Caitlin had made that there was charity in her heart, as well. Plastic surgeons had the potential of making tons of money, especially this close to Beverly Hills, but instead she'd opted to work with Doctors Without Borders.

He stepped out of the shower, vaguely surprised to discover that thoughts of Rebecca no longer held the power to bring him to his knees. The deep grief of loss had tempered to a simple sadness that at some point had become manageable.

He let go of thoughts of his dead wife and instead focused on the living, breathing Caitlin. He dressed to impress in a pair of black dress slacks and a white shirt with black and green pinstripes.

He was just about to walk out the door when his cell phone rang. He grabbed it from the bed where he'd laid it before his shower. "Agent Kane," the familiar deep voice boomed across the line.

"Sir?" Rhett instantly recognized the voice as belonging to his immediate supervisor, Kent Crawford.

"Anything to report?"

Rhett winced. "Nothing yet," he admitted.

"Does she know where her father is?"

Rhett hesitated. "I'm not sure. I'm having dinner with her tonight and hope to learn more from her. Has something happened?"

"Nothing you need to concern yourself with," Crawford replied.

From the beginning of this assignment Rhett had been on a need-to-know basis only. All he'd been told was that Mickey O'Donahue had to be found and taken into custody because he was tied to a secret society with a plot to kill the president.

Rhett didn't know what other agents were doing in an effort to find the members of the society, he didn't know who might be involved or what their involvement might be. He'd simply been assigned to come to the ranch to get whatever information he could from Mickey's daughter and get Mickey O'Donahue in custody.

"I don't have to remind you that Mickey is an integral piece of the puzzle we're trying to put together and we're depending on you to get the man into custody."

"I know, I'm working on it as fast as I can," Rhett replied.

"Work faster," Crawford replied. "We need him in custody sooner rather than later."

They spoke for several more minutes, and by the time the call ended, frustration burned in the pit of Rhett's stomach and he knew he needed to step up his game. However, as he thought of how skittish Caitlin seemed around him, he also knew he had his job cut out for him.

It was exactly six o'clock when he knocked on the front door of the house. He was surprised to feel more than a little nervous anxiety fluttering around in the pit of his stomach. He felt like a teenager on his first date, desperate that she would like him and would want to see more of him.

He needed that as an FBI agent on a mission, and he had to admit to himself that he wanted that as a man. There was nothing better for sharing secrets than pillow talk. It was definitely time for a little seduction.

Caitlin stood in front of the mirror in her bedroom, for the hundredth time cursing Esme for coming up with the idea of inviting Randall to dinner and cursing herself for agreeing to it.

There was no question that Randall Kane rattled her to the bones. There was a softness in his gaze, a softness that at times flared into something hot, something greedy that half stole her breath away.

If she'd met him two months ago she might have pursued the obvious chemistry that snapped in the air between them. Before leaving the country Caitlin had enjoyed sex, although she'd been careful in her choice of partners. She hadn't been promiscuous, but she also hadn't been a prude.

When she'd finished up her medical training, there was no question that what she'd wanted next for herself was a long-lasting relationship that included marriage and perhaps some children.

She turned away from the mirror with a sigh. Now that dream seemed as distant as the stars in the sky. She couldn't even abide the thought of a man touching her, caressing her—what were the odds she'd find love in her current state of mind?

She'd agreed to having Kane to dinner because she was lonely. She adored Esme, but the housekeeper usually ate before Caitlin, leaving Caitlin to eat her evening meal alone at the table. She and Esme had talked about everything there was to discuss and Caitlin hungered for something new, something different and, in a weak moment, she'd agreed to having Randall here for dinner.

She heard the knock on the front door and Esme's voice as she greeted their dinner guest, and nervous energy tumbled around in Caitlin's stomach. She'd thought about wearing something other than her usual jeans and T-shirt, but instantly had rebelled at the idea of dressing up for Randall Kane.

The only nod she'd given to having a guest was that she'd left her hair down around her shoulders and changed into clean jeans and a fresh navy T-shirt.

With a deep breath for courage, and a quick spritz of her favorite perfume, she went down the stairs. She smelled him before she saw him. Beneath the fragrance of the Mexican cooking, she followed the trail of his sexy cologne into the kitchen and the sight of him created a bubble of simmering energy that pressed tight against her chest.

He wore a pair of slacks as well as he did his jeans, and the dress shirt not only emphasized the broadness of his shoulders, but also did amazing things to his sexy eyes. He'd obviously taken time with his appearance and she almost wished she'd put on a dress or at least a pair of nice dress slacks instead of her usual jeans.

As he smiled at her those eyes of his slid from her head to her toes, feeling like a heated caress against her skin. "Evening," he said. "Esmeralda was just telling me she makes her own salsa and guacamole."

Caitlin nodded. "You're definitely in for a treat. Esme's tacos are an art form unto themselves." She told herself to relax, that it was just going to be a simple meal with simple conversation and nothing more.

"Caitlin's daddy loves my tacos," Esme said and her eyes suddenly welled up with tears. "I don't know why that crazy man hasn't called me. Whenever he travels he always calls me at night. I usually don't go to sleep without talking to him."

She bit her lower lip as if she'd said too much, and in that moment Caitlin was stunned to realize that Esme was in love with her father.

Esme and her father? She didn't know why she hadn't considered it before. It certainly explained why Esme hadn't left the O'Donahue household when Caitlin was grown, why she'd never had a relationship with any other man or built a family of her own.

Did Mickey feel the same way about her? Was that why Mickey had never dated? Because he had somebody at home who made him happy? *Oh, Dad, where are you?* Caitlin thought.

"I thought the two of you would enjoy eating in the dining room," Esme said, her composure quickly recovered.

"What about you?" Caitlin replied with a sense of panic.

"Oh, I've already eaten. Why don't the two of you go on in and make yourselves comfortable and I'll have the food out in no time."

Caitlin narrowed her eyes and stared at the older woman, wondering if she was attempting a little matchmaking. Esme gave her an angelic smile and then shooed them out of the kitchen.

The dining room was rarely used unless Mickey was having some of his high-powered political friends to the house. Usually meals were taken in the kitchen when it was just Caitlin, Esme and Mickey.

The ornate mahogany dining table could seat ten comfortably, but Esme had placed Caitlin and Randall across from each other at one end of the table. It was set with bright red stoneware plates, filled water glasses and two red-and-yellow bowls that held lettuce and shredded cheese.

"Would you like a drink?" Caitlin asked as she walked to the wet bar in the corner of the room. She felt as if she needed to chug a beer or two for courage.

"No, thanks. I'm not much of a drinking man," he replied.

She raised an eyebrow and looked at him curiously as she poured herself a glass of wine. "A ranch hand who doesn't enjoy a drink? I think maybe that's a first."

He smiled easily. "There was a six-month period in my life when I drank too much. I pulled myself out of the bottom of a bottle a little over seven years ago and I've never looked back."

"That's admirable, to know you have a problem and then fix it."

Those broad shoulders of his moved up and down in an easy shrug. "I don't know how admirable it was, all I knew at the time was that I had a choice to make between living and dying and I decided living was definitely more appealing."

She wanted to ask him what had happened preceding that six-month period that had plunged him into the bottom of the bottle, but she didn't want to know too much about him. Personal information might produce a false sense of intimacy that she didn't need, didn't want in her life.

"Please, sit down," she said and gestured him to the table. She had never felt so on edge, so awkward in her life.

"After you," he replied.

She was aware of his gaze intensely focused on her as she rounded the table and sat in the chair. She wanted to tell him to stop looking at her as if she were a delectable dessert he intended to savor later.

Thankfully, at that moment Esme came in carrying a serving tray that held all the rest of the toppings for the tacos. "I hope you like things spicy, Randall," she said as she placed the items in the center of the table between them.

"I'm a spicy kind of guy," he replied with an easy grin.

"I figured that the minute I laid eyes on you," Esme replied with a smile. "Caitlin has a little spicy in her, too."

Randall raised one of his eyebrows and looked at Caitlin in speculation. "I look forward to seeing that side of you sometime."

Don't hold your breath. That's what she wanted to tell him, but instead she merely started thinking of ways to kill Esme for even suggesting that Randall come to dinner. She took a sip of her wine and wished for the evening to be over.

"I'll be right back with the tacos," Esme said and disappeared into the kitchen. There was a moment of awkward silence before Esme returned, this time carrying a large platter of tacos and a bowl of Spanish rice. "I've got sopaipillas and honey for dessert."

"I think I've died and gone to heaven," Randall exclaimed. Esme giggled like a schoolgirl and then left the dining room.

"She's been with your family a long time?" Randall asked.

"For as long as I can remember. Dig in," she said.

"Your mother?" he asked as he grabbed one of the huge tacos and put it on his plate.

"Died of cancer when I was little. I was only three and have no memories of her, although my dad has told me a lot about her." Some of the tension inside her began to ebb a little. "Dad was very much a hands-on kind of father when it came to raising me, but Esme certainly helped make the job easier for him." She grabbed one of the tacos for herself. "She has been a loving, supportive part of my life."

"Does your father have a girlfriend? Maybe he's holed up someplace with a beautiful woman?"

Caitlin shook her head. "I'd know if Dad had a girlfriend. He's never shown much interest in being with anyone." Once again she thought of the look on Esme's face when she'd spoken of Mickey and wondered if Esme and her father had been in a long-term relationship.

"I was just wondering if it might have been a scorned woman who took a couple of potshots at me the other night thinking I was your father."

Caitlin focused her attention on her plate. "I find that hard to believe." What she found interesting was that he felt the same way she did, that those bullets had been meant for Mickey.

"Must have been tough being raised without a mother." She looked up to see Randall begin to build his taco.

"Not really. Mickey was as adept at painting finger-nails as he was at breaking horses or backing the right politician. I guess it's a case of you can't miss what you don't know. I had Dad and Esme and never felt a lack of anything. Tell me about your parents and life with them."

Any nervousness that had worried her disappeared as they ate and he regaled her with stories from his youth. He had a wonderful sense of humor, and as he told her outrageous stories of rodeo debacles and life with a bull-riding father and barrel-racing mother, she found her laughter again and it felt wonderful.

By the time Esme served the sopaipillas and coffee, Caitlin was more relaxed than she'd been in a month. On an intellectual level she understood that bad men had done bad things to her in the jungle, but that didn't mean all men were bad, and Randall definitely seemed to be a good man.

There was real love and respect in his voice when he talked about his parents. "What happened to them?" she finally asked, remembering that he'd told her he had no family.

"They were coming home from a rodeo late one night

and a semitruck crossed the center lane and hit them head-on. They were both killed instantly. We later found out the truck driver had fallen asleep behind the wheel."

"That's terrible," Caitlin exclaimed. "How old were you?"

"I was twenty-five."

"You must have been devastated."

"It was tough," he agreed. "I still miss them sometimes."

From there the conversation turned to favorite movies and food, places they had traveled to and life on a working ranch, and she realized they had a lot in common.

"These are absolutely amazing," he said as he drizzled honey over a second sopaipilla.

"Esme is worth her weight in gold when it comes to cooking."

"Do you cook?"

"I can, but I don't very often," she replied. "Esme insisted I learn. When I was young I was responsible for the evening meal one night a week. Esme always told me I got an A for effort and my father told me I should always make sure I had enough money to hire a cook." She smiled at the memory.

He laughed and popped the last of the sweet treat into his mouth and then sighed. "If we don't get up from this table this very minute, I'm going to sit here and eat every last one of those and then tomorrow I'll be too sick to work."

"Why don't we take our coffee into the living room," Caitlin suggested. It was still relatively early and if she were perfectly honest with herself she would admit that she was enjoying his company.

"Sounds like a plan," he agreed and grabbed his cup and stood.

Minutes later they were both seated on the leather sofa in the living room. Once again a tiny flicker of tension tried to take hold of her at his nearness. His scent surrounded her, and sitting this close to him she could see the tiny flecks of gold that made his green eyes sparkle so brightly.

"So, what are your plans now that you're back in the States?" he asked.

"I haven't thought that far ahead." She frowned thoughtfully. She felt as if she couldn't make any plans at all for herself until she found out what was going on with her father. "Things are kind of up in the air right now with my dad gone."

"Does he have friends he might be staying with?"

"None that I know of." She'd hoped he was with Hank Kelley, but Dylan would have told her if the two men were together. Dylan had known she was worried. "Hopefully he'll be calling me anytime now. We checked in with each other about once a week when I was out of the country."

"And he'll come back when he knows you're back home?"

"Definitely," she replied. She would absolutely insist her father come home no matter where on the face of the planet he was when he called. She needed him here.

She wanted answers and they had to figure out what to do about the mess he was in.

"I'm anxious to meet him. He sounds like a terrific guy." He looked at her curiously. "What did bring you home from your work? Did you know that your father had gone missing?"

"No, nothing like that. I didn't know he wasn't home until I got here." As memories of what had brought her home tried to take hold of her, she broke eye contact with him. "I just wanted to come home."

"The living conditions there must have been fairly primitive," he observed.

She nodded. "They weren't the best, but that wasn't what made me want to come home." She didn't want him to think she was some kind of a spoiled woman who couldn't put up with a little dirt and discomfort.

Still he gazed at her curiously, as if wanting to know every secret she possessed. "Did something bad happen when you were down there? Did you lose a patient or something?" His voice was soft, as if he sensed the turmoil inside her and wanted to help her ease it.

"No, nothing like that," she replied, still unable to look at him, afraid that he might see something in her eyes, something on her face that would indicate trauma. "I just got homesick," she finally answered even though she knew it was inadequate.

"Personally, I'm glad you came home."

Her gaze shot back to him to see a flirtatious smile curving his hot, sexy lips. Suddenly she wanted him gone, needed him gone because that smile of his, that shine of something just a little hungry in his eyes, both scared her and thrilled her. She was afraid that if she spent another minute with him she might tell him what had happened to her, she might want to seek comfort in his arms.

"It's getting late. We should probably call it a night," she said.

He looked at her in surprise and then glanced at his watch. She knew it was only around seven-thirty, hardly late in anyone's world, but she felt the burning need to get away from the scent of him that drew her in, the swift flutter of crazy desire he evoked, a desire that warred with a tinge of fear inside her.

"You're the boss," he said as he placed his cup on the coaster on the coffee table and then stood. "It's just been a long time since I've enjoyed a woman's company as much as I enjoy yours."

Caitlin didn't know how to reply, so she was silent as she got to her feet and together they headed for the front door. When he reached it he turned back toward her and she realized she stood far too close to him, but her feet refused to move her backward.

"Thanks for the good food and the great company," he said.

"No problem." Her voice sounded slightly breathy to her own ears.

"I really enjoyed it." He took a step toward her. His eyes shone with that hungry glaze that both disturbed and drew her in with an intoxicating power. In that moment of his nearness she knew he was going to kiss her.

Step back! A little voice screamed inside her head. *Stop it before it starts.* But her feet refused to obey her mind, and then his lips were on hers in a hot feather-soft kiss that strangely enough didn't feel threatening at all. In fact, it was more than a little bit wonderful.

It was only when his arms raised to embrace her that she felt trapped, that the birth of panic rose up inside her chest. She pushed against his chest and stepped back.

"I don't know what it is you're looking for, Randall, but you definitely won't find it here with me." Her voice trembled slightly.

"Kind of like trouble, I'm not looking for it but I'm ready for whatever comes my way." He rocked back on his heels and studied her with slightly narrowed eyes. "I like you, Caitlin, I thought you liked me and I figured we'd just let things take their natural course."

"Nothing is going to happen here with me."

"And why is that?" All trace of that simmering hunger in his eyes was gone, replaced by a still intensity.

She folded her arms in front of her chest and refused to look at him. "Because I don't like to be touched." Tears burned at her eyes and she consciously willed them away, not wanting him to see them.

"Caitlin, look at me." There was a quiet command in his voice and she found herself obeying, once again gazing at him. "If you don't like to be touched, then it's because somebody hasn't been touching you right. Good night, Caitlin."

* * *

Senator Hank Kelley sat on the edge of the bed in the bedroom he'd been sleeping in since he'd escaped to his son Cole's ranch in Maple Grove, Montana. The ranch, owned by both his twin sons, Dylan and Cole, was more like a compound, with enough high-tech security to keep anyone inside safe from outside threats.

Life as he knew it had become a never-ending nightmare. He'd had it all—a beautiful wife, attractive and successful children, and the kind of power, wealth and influence most men only dreamed of possessing.

It had all began to unravel when his mistresses started going public. Even then he hadn't been able to foresee the dangerous mess that would eventually become his life.

The women had meant nothing to him. He'd been a politician away from home for long periods of time. He'd done nothing that others hadn't done before him, wouldn't do long after he was gone—indulged in a few extramarital affairs while away from his family.

But at the moment it wasn't those women who were on his mind, it was his daughter, Lana, and the Raven's Head Society members who held her captive.

If there was one thing he held dear it was Lana, the one child who had stuck by him even when the scandals had begun to unfold. She'd been a source of love, of comfort for her father, and now she was in danger.

Hank wasn't a particularly emotional man, but as he thought of his beautiful, loving daughter in the hands of her kidnappers, tears blurred his vision.

He knew what the kidnappers wanted. They wanted him dead. They wanted him to take the responsibility for the plot to kill President Joe Colton and then kill himself, leaving them free to continue their evil.

For the thousandth time since arriving here, he tried to think rationally. If he came forward and told the authorities what he knew, then there was no question in his mind that Lana would die. Even if he did as the kidnappers asked and killed himself, there was no guarantee that they would release his daughter.

He was caught in a quagmire, unable to make a move, afraid to make a decision for fear it might be the wrong one.

He didn't even know for sure at this point whether Lana was still alive, and the agony of not knowing was horrific. He'd requested new proof of life but so far had heard nothing from the people who held her captive.

His sons didn't respect him, his daughter might be dead. Maybe the best choice *would* be for him to commit suicide. Even as he thought it, a touch of self-preservation and rebellion rose up inside him.

He was an important man. He could still do great things for the country, and he was smart. Somehow, someway, he had to figure a way out of this, a way that kept Lana safe and him still alive.

Chapter 6

Somebody had hurt her.

The words reverberated around in Rhett's head the next morning as he went about the daily chores. He didn't know who might be responsible and he didn't know when it might have happened, but there was no question in his mind that somebody had hurt Caitlin badly.

He'd wanted to push her hard last night, had planned a full-on seductive assault, but he'd tasted the panic that sprang to her lips when he'd raised his arms to embrace her. It had been fear that had momentarily darkened her eyes as she'd stumbled back from him.

Somebody had hurt her and it shouldn't affect him, but it did. He shouldn't care, but he did, and that fact bothered him more than a little bit.

He wasn't here to get enmeshed in her emotional life. He wasn't here to care about whether somebody had hurt her. He'd always found it so easy to keep his emotions out of his job. He'd always been able to maintain a healthy emotional distance, but it was definitely proving challenging with Caitlin.

He kept an eye on the house throughout the morning, hoping that she would come out, that he could glean more information on exactly what had happened to her.

Contrary to her denial, had she fallen in love with one of the doctors she'd worked with? Was it a broken heart that had brought her home, that made her not like to be touched? Or was it something darker?

And he was no closer to finding out the whereabouts of Mickey than he'd been when he'd arrived here four days ago. Tomorrow was Saturday. Hopefully Mickey would come home and Rhett could get him under arrest and leave before he got too much more emotionally involved with the man's daughter.

And he *was* getting emotionally invested in Caitlin, something he definitely hadn't planned. Maybe it was a signal that he had truly put Rebecca's death behind him.

Despite everything that was on his mind, he found himself relaxing as he went about the chores. He'd always loved ranch life and working with animals. Even the most mundane task felt peaceful and right and reminded him of everything he'd given up when Rebecca had died.

By the time lunchtime came Caitlin still hadn't made

an appearance, and as he went into his cabin to eat something he wondered if maybe he'd pushed too hard, come on too strong the night before and ruined any chance he might have had to get close to her.

He ate quickly, eager to get back outside in case Caitlin decided to venture out. He told himself his desire to see her, to spend time with her was nothing more than his need to do his job. He didn't have to sleep with her to get close to her, he reasoned.

He didn't have to touch her, although he had to admit his fingers itched with the need to stroke the smoothness of her fair skin and to feel the silky softness of her hair. She was becoming a burn in his stomach that wouldn't go away, an itch that needed to be scratched by her alone.

He finished eating and went back outside to see fellow ranch hand Clint Gregory leading a saddled Buttercup out of the stables.

"What's up?" he asked Clint.

"The boss lady called me on my cell phone and told me to saddle up Buttercup for her." He tied the horse on a nearby fence post and then leaned against the railing and gave Rhett a friendly smile. "I noticed the oat hay out in the pasture. I told Garrett a million times that the horses were getting too thin but he wouldn't listen to me."

"From what I've heard, Simms didn't do much of anything around here except get his nose in the sauce."

"You got that right," Clint agreed. "Half the time he was on the property he was drunk as a skunk. Mickey tried to fire him half a dozen times but Garrett would always cry like a little girl and say he didn't have any place else to go. Thank God you're here and Garrett isn't coming back. It was past time for a change."

"What's Mickey O'Donahue like?" Rhett asked, figuring the more information he had about the man the better.

"A good boss. Fair and decent. He can ride a horse better than anyone I've ever seen. Got a bit of a temper on him, but usually when he blows it's because he has good cause." Clint's eyes narrowed slightly. "I've noticed you and Caitlin hanging around with each other a lot. A friendly word of warning, Mickey adores his daughter, and if you trifle with her, he'll have your head on a stick and you won't be able to find work anywhere in the state of California."

"Point taken," Rhett replied. Of course, there was no way he could not "trifle" with Caitlin. Ultimately he knew the consequences of his relationship with Caitlin had disaster written all over them, but he couldn't think about that now. Besides, it would be difficult for Mickey to "blow" too bad in handcuffs.

Both men turned at the sound of the front door opening. Caitlin stepped out onto the porch and Rhett instantly felt a coil of heat unfurl in his stomach.

As usual she was dressed in a pair of tight jeans and the bright yellow T-shirt was a perfect foil to the flaming color of her hair. As she stepped off the porch and approached them, Rhett thought of that moment the night before when his mouth had touched hers.

Her lips had been hot and sweet, as if they'd retained some of the honey she'd eaten on the sopaipillas. For just a brief instant he'd felt her respond to him, her lips yielding beneath his in acquiescence. If she hadn't stopped him when she had, there was no doubt he would have swept her up in his arms, carried her up to her bedroom and made love to her.

"Good morning, Clint…Randall," she said as she reached them. Her gaze didn't quite meet Rhett's and he wondered if she, too, was remembering the brief kiss they'd shared the night before.

Both Rhett and Clint greeted her. "Heading out for a ride?" Rhett asked, stating the obvious. She nodded, still not looking at him. "Need some company?" he asked.

"Not this time." Her gaze finally connected with his. "I'm looking forward to a solitary ride."

Rhett thought he'd taken two steps forward with her the night before, but he now suspected it had put him two steps back. There was a distance in her eyes, a rigid tension in her body as she mounted Buttercup.

"Have a good ride," Clint said and then with a wave of his hand he ambled back toward the stables.

"I enjoyed last night," Rhett said to her, an attempt to break through the distance he felt between them.

Her features softened slightly. "I enjoyed it, too." She said the words as if she were confessing to something heinous.

"Did you sleep well?" He knew she was eager to take off, but he wanted somehow to break through the distance he sensed coming from her.

"I slept fine. I'll be back later." With a cluck of her tongue she urged Buttercup forward.

Rhett watched her head toward the pasture, the sun sparking on her hair and her shoulders rigidly set once again.

She was definitely a mystery he wanted to solve. It was tragic that a woman who looked like her didn't want to be touched. And yet he could have sworn that more than once he'd felt a yearning emanating from her—the desire to be held by him.

Talk about mixed signals. With a frustrated sigh he turned away and walked toward the small corral. If he couldn't use this time to gentle Caitlin, then he'd work on Molly.

The explosion of two gunshots, one right after the other, whirled Rhett around in his tracks. As Clint came running out of the stable, Rhett looked out in the distance and saw Buttercup running wildly across the pasture and a splash of yellow on the ground, lying motionless.

Horror gripped Rhett by the throat as he was instantly cast back to another place, another time. The horse running wild…the broken, unmoving woman on the ground… Visions from the past ripped through him as he took off running, all rational thought gone from his head.

As he raced across the pasture, he was vaguely aware of Clint's voice shouting behind him, but Rhett's only thoughts were for the woman lying so motionless on the ground.

His heart crashed inside him as he raced ahead. If he could just get to her in time he could make everything okay. If help came quickly enough she could live and their lives would go on as they had been. Hurry, hurry!

In his mind it wasn't an autumn day but rather a brisk spring morning in Wyoming. He and Rebecca had enjoyed an early breakfast and then had decided on a ride. They'd saddled up and as they took off he'd challenged her to a race, as they'd done so many mornings in their past.

"Rebecca." Her name left his lips on a cry of agony and it was only when he saw Caitlin's red hair that the present slammed back in and rational thought returned.

Gunshots. He'd definitely heard gunshots.

He fell to the ground and grabbed his gun, his heart pounding a million beats a minute as reality set in.

Somebody had shot at her. Somebody had shot at Caitlin. Was she hit?

Was she dead?

She lay on her side facing away from him about twenty feet in front of him. He couldn't tell if she was breathing or not. He surveyed the vicinity, assuming that the shooter had been hiding in the stand of trees off to the left of the pasture. Was he still there? Waiting to see if he'd killed her? Waiting to try again?

He became aware of Clint crawling up to his side, the man also holding a revolver in his hand. "What the hell is going on?" he said.

"I don't know, but she may be badly hurt. I need to

get to her," Rhett said, his focus on the fallen Caitlin. "But I think the shooter is someplace in those trees."

"I'll head that way, you get to her," Clint replied tersely. Staying low to the ground, he headed for the trees while Rhett moved forward and prayed that Caitlin wasn't hurt too badly.

"Caitlin," he said softly as he approached her. "Caitlin, can you hear me?" *Please, let her be alive. Let her at least be conscious,* he thought.

She rolled over on her back as he reached her. He nearly sobbed in relief as he saw that there was no blood staining her shirt, no visible signs of injury. Her eyes were wide and filled with unadulterated fear.

"I'm okay," she finally gasped. "He missed me but I knew I was a sitting duck on Buttercup's back so I jumped off and hit the ground."

"Smart woman," Rhett muttered. He didn't even want to think what might have happened if she hadn't bailed off her horse.

By that time two of the other ranch hands came riding out on horseback, both of them armed with shotguns and obviously ready to help. As Jimmy Mathis headed toward the trees, Larry Tredwell reined up beside Rhett and Caitlin.

Larry was a big, burly man with arms the size of tree trunks. "Let's get her up in front of you on the horse so you can get her back to the house," Rhett said. He figured if Caitlin was seated in front of Larry, then Larry's big body would provide as much safety as possible.

It took only a minute for Caitlin to get on the horse

and for Larry to gallop off toward the house. Only then did Rhett release a sigh of relief. But his relief was short-lived as his brain worked to process what had just happened.

He'd thought the bullets that had whacked into the front door the other night had been intended for Mickey, that the shooting had been a case of mistaken identity.

There was no way this had been the same kind of deal. The shooter couldn't have mistaken Caitlin, with her female physique and that brilliant hair, for anyone other than who she was—so the question was, why was somebody trying to kill Caitlin?

As he headed toward the trees he realized this changed everything. If what he suspected was true, then there had been not one, but two attempts on Caitlin's life. *Third time is a charm,* he thought grimly. He had to make sure there was no third time.

Minutes later Jimmy Mathis rode out of the trees, followed by Clint on foot. "We found a place where the shooter might have been standing, but whoever it was is gone now," Jimmy said as he reined up next to Rhett.

"What the hell is going on around here?" Clint asked as he joined them. "Who would want to hurt Caitlin?"

"I don't know, but I'm going to do my damnedest to figure it out," Rhett replied. "In the meantime I want you all to keep your eyes open for anyone on the property who doesn't belong."

"Shoot first and ask questions later, that's what I say," Jimmy said, his brown eyes glittering darkly as he shifted his weight in his saddle.

"Just make sure the person stays in good enough condition to answer some questions later," Rhett replied. "I'm heading to the house to check on Caitlin. I'd like you all to do a sweep of the area, and if you find anyone, bring them to me at the house."

As the men took off, Rhett headed toward the house, the beat of his heart finally slowing to a more normal pace, but he knew that if he focused on that moment of Caitlin lying so still on the ground, his heart would ramp up to warp speed again.

The game had just changed and the stakes were higher than ever before.

Two failed attempts on Caitlin's life led him to believe there would be another attempt. He had to make sure that one was equally unsuccessful. His mind whirled with each step he took as he tried to figure out the best way to proceed from here.

His ultimate goal was still to find Mickey, but his immediate goal was to make sure that Caitlin stayed safe. And there was only one way he knew to do that… whether she liked it or not, Caitlin was about to get a roommate.

Caitlin sat on the sofa, Esme buzzing around her like a bothersome fly. "Are you cold? I could get you a blanket," Esme said as she stood inches from Caitlin and wrung her hands together. "Do you need something to eat? Or tea…maybe you need a nice hot cup of tea?"

"Yes, tea," Caitlin replied quickly, just wanting to

give Esme something to do that would allow Caitlin time to breathe, a minute to think.

"I'll be right back," Esme said and hurried into the kitchen.

Caitlin leaned back in the leather sofa and fought against a shiver that threatened to waltz up her back as she thought of how close death had come.

She'd felt the whiz of the bullets as they'd shot past her head. For an instant she hadn't known what they were, but when the realization struck her, she'd bailed off Buttercup and hugged the ground, hoping she would be a more difficult target that way.

God, she'd been so afraid, was still so afraid. Somebody had tried to kill her. Although the words whirled around and around in her brain, she couldn't quite make sense of them.

Her knee ached from where she'd hit the ground, but that pain was minor compared to the fear that now gripped her heart. If she hadn't jumped off Buttercup when she did there was no question in her mind that a third bullet would have slammed into her. She would have been killed.

What was happening around here? Did this have something to do with her father? Had the evil from the jungle somehow followed her home?

The shiver she'd worked so hard to suppress shuddered through her with icy fingers just as Rhett walked into the living room. His lips were compressed in a grim line that merely served to remind her how close she'd been to death.

"You okay?" he asked.

She started to assure him that she was fine, but before the reassuring words could leave her lips an unexpected sob escaped instead. In three long strides he was in front of her.

Before she could protest he had her up off the sofa and in a tight embrace that nearly stole her breath away. Instinctively she felt the need to struggle at his closeness, but as her tears came faster the instinct faded away and instead she leaned weakly against him, welcoming the strong arms that held her tight.

She was vaguely surprised that she didn't feel trapped, but rather safe with her body so close to his. She needed to be held as the shuddering fear washed through her.

"It's all right," he whispered softly against her hair. "You're fine and I'm not going to let anyone hurt you. It's going to be okay, Caitlin, you're going to be okay."

She welcomed the words of comfort even though she wasn't sure she truly believed them. For several long moments she stood in his arms, oddly reluctant to leave his embrace.

Finally, with a gulping gasp, she staunched any tears that might try to follow the initial torrent and stepped away from him.

"I'm sorry," she said as she swiped the moisture off her cheeks. "I don't usually break down like that." She sank back down on the sofa, afraid that her trembling legs wouldn't hold her up another minute without his support. "I'm just so scared."

He nodded. "I've got the men checking out the area to make sure nobody is on the property who isn't supposed to be." He sat down next to her as Esme came back in with a cup of tea.

"Randall," she said as she set the tea on the coffee table in front of Caitlin. "What in heaven's name is happening around here? Somebody shot at Caitlin. You have to find out who is responsible for this."

"I'm going to do the best that I can, but I'll tell you one thing, the two of you aren't staying in this house alone for another minute. I'm moving in."

He looked at Caitlin, his chin lifted as if expecting a protest. But the protest he expected, the one Caitlin was sure would spew out of her, didn't come.

She realized she wanted him beneath this roof until they knew what was happening. She didn't want to be alone with just Esme in the house. Somebody obviously had a problem with her, and until she knew who and why, she wasn't taking any foolish chances.

"We'll put him in the guest room next to mine," she said to the older woman.

Esme nodded. "I'll go upstairs and get it ready." As Esme disappeared up the stairs, Caitlin turned to look back at Rhett. There was a touch of surprise on his ruggedly handsome features.

"I might be strong-willed and independent, but I'm not stupid enough to turn down help when it's offered," she said wryly.

"I'll keep that in mind," he replied, some of the darkness in his eyes lifting.

"That night on the porch, somebody tried to shoot me then, too." It wasn't a question but rather a statement of fact as she thought of that surprise attack.

"That would be my assessment now," he agreed. "And this is when I ask you again if you have any enemies that I need to know about."

She shook her head and felt the press of tears burning hot behind her eyes once again. "No, I can't imagine what this is all about." God, she needed to talk to her father and she needed to forget that for just a few minutes she'd liked the feel of Rhett's arms around her.

"I feel as though my head is about to explode with so many questions and I don't know where to go to get answers," she finally said.

"I'm going to head out to my cabin and pack up my things. I'll be back here in fifteen minutes or so and then maybe we can put our heads together and figure something out." He got up from the sofa. "Walk me to the door and lock it behind me."

She pulled herself up off the sofa and walked with him to the door. As he stepped outside she shut and locked the door, then moved to a window where she could see him as he walked toward the foreman's cabin.

She'd been stunned to realize that she'd wanted him to hold her, that she'd wanted his strong arms wrapped around her as he told her everything was going to be fine.

Of course, standing in a man's embrace for a few moments was far different than making love with him. Just because she'd found comfort in Randall's arms for a minute didn't mean there could ever be anything else between them.

It had to be terror that had made her feel more than okay in his arms. She'd just suffered a tremendous shock and any strong arms would have done the trick.

Still, there was no question that she'd feel safer with him in the house. This had shaken her to her bones, made her wonder where danger might come from next.

She turned as Esme touched her on the back. "The room is ready for him."

Caitlin turned to face her. "Are you in love with my father?" she asked, desperate to focus on anything other than bullets and Randall.

Esme's cheeks flamed bright red and her gaze quickly skittered from Caitlin's. "What would make you say such a thing? Somebody just tried to kill you and you're wondering about my love life?"

"I think I have my answer in the redness of your blush," Caitlin replied gently. "It's okay, Esme. If you and my father have a relationship I'm happy about it."

Esme's gaze met hers and she released a tremulous sigh. "I think I fell in love with your father on the day he hired me to take care of you, but he was nothing but an employer for many years."

She grabbed Caitlin's hand in hers. "Your father, he grieved deep and long for your mother. She was the love of his life, and it took him many years before he was able to move past his grief. You were in college when things changed between me and Mickey. We realized that we cared about each other. He's my heart, Caitlin, and I believe that I have become his."

Wistfulness filled Caitlin, along with a sweet happiness at knowing that the two people she loved most in the world had found each other. "But why haven't the two of you married?" she asked.

Esme dropped her hand. "Your father asked me to marry him years ago, but I told him no. He's an important man and I am his housekeeper. I never wanted to be a liability for him. I'm satisfied with the way things are." Her eyes darkened. "But we need him home now more than ever. I'm afraid for you, Caitlin, but I'm afraid for him, too. Why hasn't he called?"

Caitlin wished she had the answer. "I don't know," she finally said. At that moment there was a knock on the door signaling that Randall had returned with his things.

Caitlin let him in and her mind was once again filled with the thought of the whiz of bullets and the warm safety of Randall's arms. He carried only the duffel bag she'd seen in his room. Obviously a man who traveled light, she thought.

"I'll show you to your room," she said.

He nodded and followed her as she headed up the stairs. There was a part of her that wondered if having him in the house, right next door to her bedroom, wasn't a mistake.

What if he heard her scream during one of her nightmares? What if he wanted to know what those dreams were about? What if she found herself in his arms once again? It would definitely be false advertising on her part. She already knew he felt desire for her, and to lead him on in any way wouldn't be fair to either of them.

"Here you are," she said as she led him into the guest bedroom decorated in shades of navy blue and ivory. The bed was king-size and the nightstands and dresser a dark mahogany. "There's a bathroom across the hall and everything you need should be in the linen closet."

He dropped the duffel bag to the floor and offered her a warm smile. "Definitely beats the foreman's quarters." The smile lasted only a moment and then was replaced with a small grimace. "I talked to the men. They checked the property but didn't see anyone. They found an area in the trees where they think the shooter stood to fire at you, but nothing to indicate who or why."

Caitlin's knee began to throb and a headache blossomed across the front of her forehead. She raised her hands and rubbed her temples. "I can't imagine why any of this is happening."

"Headache?" he asked, a touch of sympathy in his gaze.

She nodded. "I think maybe I'm starting to feel the effects of hitting the ground from Buttercup's back."

"Not to mention the whole emotional trauma of being shot at. I'd say that's enough to give anyone a headache. Why don't you take a hot bath, maybe lie down for a little while? Consider me officially on duty as your bodyguard."

Her bodyguard. She definitely liked the sound of that. She gave him a grateful smile. She had no idea what winds of fate had blown him to this ranch, to her, but she was aware of the fact that he was going above and beyond his job for her.

"I think maybe I'll do just that," she said. "I'll see you later for dinner." She left him in the guest room and went to her own room and closed the door.

Heading for her bathroom, she stripped as she walked, her thoughts consumed by the man in the room next door. In the span of three short days he'd made her not only like him, but trust him, as well.

There was something so solid, so reassuring about him. There was something so hot and tempting, as well. She got into the shower and stepped beneath the warm spray of water.

Somebody had tried to kill her. There was no way to sugarcoat what had happened in the pasture. Those had been real bullets that had buzzed by her head, with the real capacity to take her out of this world.

Who? Who had tried to kill her and why? There had to be a reason for somebody to want her dead, but damned if she knew what it might be. Whoever it was had tried twice already. When and from where would another attempt occur? She shivered despite the hot water that cascaded over her bare skin.

They should call the police to report the shooting. Esme had wanted to, but Caitlin had talked her out of it. She was afraid to get the police involved in any way until she knew what kind of trouble her father might be in. Besides, she consoled herself with the fact that Rhett was here and he would do everything in his power to protect her. For the moment, until she knew more about her father's circumstances, that had to be enough.

It was much easier to think about Esme and her father. She should be shocked by what Esme had told her, but she wasn't. She now remembered stumbling down the stairs for breakfast while visiting from college to find her father and Esme sitting together drinking coffee and laughing at some private joke.

Small touches, secretive smiles, they had all been there between the two, but Caitlin hadn't been paying attention. She was glad they had each other, although she couldn't deny the hint of loneliness that filled her own soul.

She wanted what they had, a love, a devotion that would last through the years, but that dream seemed impossible now. It had been stolen from her. She shut off the water, stepped out of the shower and grabbed a towel to dry off.

Was it possible the attacks on her were somehow related to the Raven's Head Society and whatever trouble her father was in? And dammit, where was her father? Why hadn't they heard from him?

She pulled a robe around herself and got into bed, as weary as she'd ever been. The trauma of the near-death experience, coupled with the chaos in her brain, had her positively exhausted.

Surely she'd feel better after a short nap. She closed her eyes and tried to shut off her mind, but it refused to be silent.

First the men in the jungle and the attack. *Tell your*

father his old friends say hello. And now bullets flying in her direction.

Her father's absence, his very silence felt ominous. Her eyes snapped open and dread seeped into her bones. Perhaps there was a reason Mickey hadn't gotten in touch with anyone. Maybe the men who were looking for him had already found him. Her heart cried out with denial.

Maybe he was already dead.

Chapter 7

The minute Caitlin went into her room, Rhett got busy. He spent the next hour going from room to room in the large house, checking windows to make sure they were locked and doors to see if they had dead bolts. He needed to make sure the house was as secure as it could possibly be.

He was pleased to find out that the house was wired with a high-tech security system, although Esmeralda told him it was rarely used. That was about to change.

He then made a call to his supervisor to let him know what had happened. Both men speculated on whether it was possible that the attacks on Caitlin were somehow related to the Raven's Head Society, but in the end they came up with nothing conclusive.

Caitlin's relationship with her father was such that

surely the members of the society knew that if they killed Caitlin, Mickey would become a loose cannon that they couldn't control.

With his daughter dead there would be nothing to keep him from coming forward and spilling his guts. Bent on revenge, reeling with grief, he'd name names, to hell with the consequences.

Unless Mickey was already dead.

Rhett couldn't know for sure, but he didn't think the man was dead. If he was, then why would anyone go after Caitlin? He felt as if he was thinking in circles and that somehow he was missing a vital piece of information that would make it all make sense.

After the phone call he drifted down to the kitchen where Esmeralda was in the process of making dinner. "Something smells good," he said as he sat on a chair at the table.

"Pot roast and potatoes," she replied. "I just made some coffee. Would you like a cup?"

"That sounds good," he agreed.

She took down two cups from the cabinet, filled both of them and then carried them to the table where she sat across from him.

"Thank you for stepping up to try to protect Caitlin," she said. She wrapped her hands around her cup. "I just wish I knew what was going on. I wish Mickey were here."

"That makes two of us," Rhett replied.

"You like her." It was a statement, not a question.

"I do," he said not bothering to pretend he didn't

know who she was talking about. He took a sip of the coffee.

Esmeralda frowned. "She's changed. The sparkle in her eyes is gone. Something bad happened to her that brought her home, but she won't talk to me. Maybe she'll talk to you?" She eyed him hopefully.

Rhett lowered his cup. "It's doubtful. She seems fairly closed off."

Esmeralda leaned forward. "But that's not like her. Before she left to go to El Salvador she was filled with laughter and life. She left here a happy, vital woman and she came back here a dead woman with shadows in her eyes."

She certainly hadn't felt like a dead woman when he'd touched his mouth to hers. She definitely hadn't felt dead when he'd held her in his arms.

"I'm scared for her and I'm scared for Mickey," she added. "I can't imagine what's keeping him from us."

"Was he in some sort of trouble before he left here?" Rhett asked. "Maybe having a beef with somebody or having financial troubles?"

"I don't know. I don't think so, but if he was I don't think he would have told me. Mickey is old-school about those things. He'd want to protect me and Caitlin."

"Can you think of anyone Mickey might go to? Someplace he would run to if he were in trouble?" Rhett asked.

She shook her head. "No. I've racked my brains to try to figure out where he might be, why he hasn't called, but I don't have any answers."

Rhett stifled a sigh of frustration. He had no doubt that Esmeralda was telling him the truth, but he still wasn't sure what Caitlin knew or didn't know about the conspiracy her father had gotten himself involved in.

"What are you going to do to keep my girl safe?" Esmeralda asked, pulling him from his thoughts.

"Whatever I can," he replied firmly. "She's definitely not leaving this house again until we figure out who is after her. We need to make sure the doors remain locked at all times and the security system is engaged. Nobody comes into this house unless it's Mickey O'Donahue himself."

"That's fine by me." Esmeralda's dark eyes brimmed with tears. "All I want is my family safe."

Rhett's heart constricted a bit. He was betraying Esmeralda as much as he was Caitlin. The minute Mickey showed up here safe and sound, Rhett's job was to take him into custody. He had no idea what kind of charges the man would face or what kind of prison time, if any, Mickey might be looking at. What he did know was that in doing his job he was going to break the hearts of two special women.

In the past few years of his life he knew he'd broken hearts. He'd dated a little, slept with some knowing that he'd never allow himself to care deeply about any woman again. Still, the idea of breaking Esmeralda's and Caitlin's hearts weighed heavily in his mind.

As Esmeralda got up from the table to check on the evening meal, Rhett finished his coffee and then called

Clint on his cell phone and told him to meet him on the front porch.

"I want you to take over my duties as foreman for the time being," Rhett told the man as they stood on the porch minutes later. "I'm going to be staying here in the house until we figure out who tried to hurt Caitlin."

"You sure you know what you're doing? Getting personally involved in all this?" Clint asked. "If things somehow go bad it will be your head that will roll."

"No, I definitely don't know what I'm doing and I'm hoping things won't go bad," Rhett replied with a wry smile. "But there's no question that I don't want two women alone in the house after what happened this afternoon. Anybody you know have a beef with Caitlin? Maybe one of the other ranch hands?"

Clint frowned. "Not that I'm aware of and I can't imagine why anyone would have a problem with her. She hasn't been around for a while, and even before she left she wasn't a difficult woman to work for." He hesitated a moment, and then added, "Maybe somebody should check on Garrett Simms."

Rhett wanted to kick himself for not thinking about the missing foreman before now. But it seemed a stretch to think that a man would kill an innocent woman because he was unhappy at his job.

"I want you all to keep your eyes open," Rhett continued. His gaze drifted out toward the small corral where Molly was contained. "And spend some extra time with Molly."

"You got it," Clint agreed.

There was nothing more to say. The minute Clint left, Rhett called his contact and requested that somebody find Garrett Simms and check his alibi for both shootings.

After making the call Rhett went back into the house. As he walked back into the living room he saw Caitlin coming down the stairs.

She flashed him a smile that didn't reach her eyes. "Everything okay?" she asked.

"Fine," he assured her, wishing he could take the edge of fear out of her eyes. "I just spoke with Clint." He quickly recapped the conversation he'd just had. "He's a good man. He'd make a good foreman."

She looked at him sharply. "But you aren't planning on going anywhere anytime soon, right?"

"I'm not planning on going anywhere." The lie left a bitter taste in his mouth. "Did you sleep at all?"

"For a little while," she said as she sank down on the sofa. He sat in the chair opposite her, trying to forget how she'd felt in his arms, needing somehow to distance himself from her and trying to forget the lie he'd just told her.

He'd thought he was going to sweep in here, give her a taste of his charm and seduce her right into bed where she would spill the information he needed, and then he'd get Mickey and be gone.

He'd figured he could get into her bed, into her head and not get emotionally involved with her. What was going to happen to her when he left here? How would he be able to walk away from here if they hadn't figured out who wanted her dead?

At that moment Esmeralda told them dinner was ready and they moved into the kitchen. The food was delicious, the conversation almost nonexistent. It was as if they had all retreated into their own heads, they were all talked out after the long, traumatic day.

Rhett wished he could tell both of the women that he had a clue as to who had shot at Caitlin, that he had a lead he could follow that would take them to the guilty party. But he was as much in the dark as they appeared to be. He didn't mention Garrett Simms. There was no point discussing the man as a suspect until he heard back from his contacts.

Although he wasn't completely discounting the man as a suspect, his gut instinct told him the drunken foreman didn't have the brains or the follow-through to try to kill anyone, but until he was ruled out, he was still on the list—the very short list—of potential suspects.

It was as they were finishing up that Esmeralda mentioned she didn't feel well, that the stress of the day had given her a sick headache.

"Go rest," Caitlin said. "I'll clean up the kitchen."

"And I'll help her," Rhett said before Esmeralda could protest.

"Thank you," Esmeralda replied quietly. "If you both don't mind then I'll just call it a night and see you in the morning."

As she left the kitchen to head to her private quarters

at the back of the house, Caitlin got up from the table and began to clear the dishes. Rhett jumped up to help.

"Hope she'll be all right," he said as he carried a couple of plates to the sink where she had started rinsing and placing items in the dishwasher.

"She's worried and she always makes herself sick when she worries too much." She took the plates from him and dunked them into the sink full of soapy water. "I just found out this afternoon that she and my father have been a couple for years."

He raised an eyebrow. "How did that make you feel?"

"Surprised…and oddly relieved. I always worried about Dad, about him being alone when I eventually moved out of here. There's a lot of comfort for me in knowing that through the years he's had Esme to love and support him."

They fell silent as they finished the cleanup. "You want coffee or something?" she asked when the kitchen was once again clean.

"No, I'm good," he replied.

"If you don't mind I think I'll have glass of wine."

He smiled at her. "I don't have a problem with that." It touched him that she'd thought of him, remembering that he'd told her there had been a time in his life when he'd drunk too much.

He watched as she poured a glass of white wine and then together they left the kitchen and went into the living room. She sat on one end of the sofa and he sat on the other, an uncomfortable silence growing between them.

He searched his mind for something to say, but seated this close to her his thoughts were dizzied by the sweet, clean scent of her. Her hair sparkled in the overhead light as if begging him to touch the silky strands. As he remembered the brief kiss he'd stolen from her he wanted another and another.

His desire for her was not only out of character, but damned stupid. He'd always had a guarded heart, but somehow Caitlin was pulling down the barriers and that both excited and scared the hell out of him.

"You want the TV on?" she asked, finally breaking what had become an awkward silence.

"Only if you do." There was a formal politeness between them that felt unnatural, but he didn't know how to fix it.

"I really don't feel like watching anything," she replied. She took a sip of her wine and then carefully placed the glass on the coffee table. "What I'd really like to know is who Rebecca is."

Shock coursed through him as the familiar name fell unexpectedly from her mouth.

Caitlin gazed at Randall in curiosity. Even though she'd been half-wild with fear when she'd hit the ground to stop herself from being an easy target, she'd heard him call out the name *Rebecca* as he'd raced toward her.

There had been such anguish in his voice, such a depth of emotion, that it had resonated through her, and although she wanted the details, she suspected Rebecca was the woman who had made Randall decide to travel forever light and alone.

His eyes were dark as he held her gaze. "Rebecca was my wife. Eight years ago she died in my arms after being thrown from a horse." His voice was flat, emotionless despite the emotion that shone from his eyes.

Although Caitlin had thought her own feelings were dead, she tasted his grief in her mouth, felt the ache of his loss in her heart. "Oh, Randall, I'm so sorry."

He got up from the sofa and walked to the window and stared out, as if wanting to look at the shadows of twilight instead of at her.

"She was my high-school sweetheart. We got married two weeks after we graduated and moved into a tacky little apartment so we could save our money for the ranch of our dreams."

He paused, and she didn't know if he expected her to say something or not, but she had no words to give him and he turned around to face her and continued.

"It took us five years to finally save up enough for a down payment. It wasn't the ranch of our dreams, but it was a start." Some of the darkness had ebbed from his eyes. "We figured we'd work the ranch, save our money and then in another couple of years buy a bigger place and start a family."

"But you never got the chance," Caitlin said softly.

He drew in a deep breath of air and shook his head. He returned to the sofa and sank down, his eyes going to the wall just above Caitlin's head.

"It was our habit when the weather was nice to start

the day with a ride around the pasture." His gaze once again connected with hers and in his eyes she saw the sadness that she could only guess had become an intrinsic part of him. "That morning I challenged her to a race."

The words held the hollow ring of guilt and Caitlin tensed as she waited for him to tell the rest of the story, as she waited to hear about the moment his life had changed forever.

"We'd raced a hundred times before—sometimes I beat her, sometimes she'd win." A whisper of a smile curved his lips. "And when she won, she didn't let me live it down. She'd crow about it for the rest of the day." The smile vanished from his mouth and once again he got up from the sofa and moved back to the window as if unable to sit any longer.

"I took off galloping across the pasture, laughing as I realized I easily had the lead. I reached a grove of trees that was always the end of the race and turned around."

She couldn't see his face, but his back was rigid and his voice was filled with emotion suppressed so tightly she suspected an explosion was imminent.

"I don't know what happened. I'll never know exactly what happened. She never made a sound, never cried out, but when I turned around I saw Rebecca's horse running wild and Rebecca was crumpled on the ground not moving."

He paused and drew a deep breath, and Caitlin realized that when he'd seen her on the ground that afternoon his mind had flashed him back in time; that explained why he'd called his wife's name.

"I ran to her and instantly I knew it was bad," he continued. "She was unconscious and her back was twisted in a way that told me it had to be broken. I used my cell phone to call for help and then I crouched next to her and waited for help to come. It didn't come in time. She never regained consciousness, and within minutes I felt the life leave her body."

He fell silent, but didn't move away from the window. It was Caitlin who found herself on her feet, her heart aching with his pain. She walked to him, for a moment afraid to touch him, afraid that if she did touch him he'd shatter into a million pieces.

And yet she couldn't not touch him. They were alike—both with dreams of happily ever after shattered by events beyond their control. She'd never felt as close to him as she did at this moment, with the weight of his tragedy so heavy in her heart.

Hesitantly she reached out her hand. Did he need her touch as badly as she wanted to touch him? She splayed her hand on the center of his back and felt the taut muscles and the warmth of his skin radiating through his shirt.

He turned to face her and she allowed her arm to drop to her side. "That's why I don't stay in one place for too long. I swore the day that I buried Rebecca that I'd never allow myself to care that deeply about anyone again."

Emotion thrust itself up inside her. His pain was hers,

his shattered dreams mirrored her own, and she couldn't stop the tears that blurred her vision. His story had made her feel for the first time since the jungle.

"Don't cry," he said softly. "It was a long time ago."

She nodded her head, but the tears came faster and faster. She found herself pulled against his chest, his arms wrapped around her as she sobbed into the front of his shirt.

She felt ridiculous, but realized she was wildly out of control and didn't know how to regain it. She knew she should step away from him, but instead she clung with her arms around his shoulders and her body pressed tight against his as she continued to weep.

She'd lost her very soul and he'd lost the woman he'd apparently loved as much as life itself. They were both tragic victims of a cruel fate. He'd survived his trauma and she was still struggling to survive hers.

Finally the tears slowed and then stopped and still she remained in the warmth of his embrace. She raised her head to look at him. "I'm normally not a weepy kind of woman. I don't know what's wrong with me."

The sadness that had been in his eyes was gone, replaced by a warmth that torched through her. "Maybe it has something to do with the fact that you don't know where your father is and somebody tried to kill you today. I think that would make me a weepy kind of man."

A small bubble of laughter escaped her and once again she told herself she should move out of his arms, but her body refused to obey her mental command.

His eyes deepened in hue, becoming a smoke of desire as he continued to look at her. "Caitlin, I'm going to kiss you now." He hesitated a moment, as if giving her time to protest what he was about to do.

A million butterflies took flight in the pit of her stomach and a tremor of anticipation swept through her. *Tell him no,* a little voice whispered inside her head. "Okay," she heard herself say.

His mouth lightly touched hers in a tender kiss that swept away any protest she might have made. She didn't feel threatened, she didn't feel trapped. Rather, a sharp edge of desire rose up inside her.

She felt herself relaxing against him, her breasts sinking against his broad chest, her heart beating against his as she opened her mouth to allow him to deepen the kiss.

His tongue touched the tip of hers, tentative as if exploring his welcome. She swirled her tongue with his, a welcomed heat searing through her as the kiss continued.

He kissed with a masterful command, as if he enjoyed kissing and was determined that she would, too. And she did. She loved the way his mouth felt against hers, the hot hunger that sparked in his lips.

Maybe she wasn't as damaged as she'd thought. Hope buoyed inside her at the thought. Maybe she could make love to a man and not feel sick, not experience the bone-chilling terror of that agonizing time in the jungle.

When he finally broke the kiss his gaze remained hot and hungry. "I want you, Caitlin."

The stark, simple words evoked a new shiver of apprehension…and of want…inside her. If she was going to find out whether she was capable of making love again, she wanted it to be with him.

Even though she'd only known him for a brief period of time, she felt she knew him as well as she'd known anyone she'd ever made love with before. She knew the kind of heart he possessed, a wounded one that still had the capacity to care for a traumatized horse, that still had the ability to offer himself up as bodyguard to a woman in trouble.

"I want you, too." The words whispered out of her and she didn't know if she was frightened or excited. She only knew her words had placed into motion something she wanted…needed and yet was ultimately terrified of what might happen.

"Are we going to do something about it or are we just going to stand here and talk about it?" he asked. He dropped his arms from around her and took a step back. "It's your call, Caitlin. I don't want you to do anything that you don't want to. You know that I'm not the kind of man to stick around forever."

For some reason that made it easier on her. He wouldn't be around forever, and if things went terribly wrong neither of them had anything invested in each other.

He held out his hand to her and she knew that if she placed her hand in his he'd lead her upstairs to her bedroom. She wanted that…and she was afraid of that.

Still, there was a softness in his eyes that reassured

her. This was a man who knew gentleness, a man she trusted implicitly.

She placed her hand in his and together they headed up the stairs. Between the stairs and the threshold of her room, she changed her mind a hundred times. But by the time they entered her room and he pulled her back into his arms and took her lips once again in a kiss, her desire had overridden her fear.

It's going to be okay, she told herself as the kiss grew deeper, hungrier. Even when his hands slid up beneath the bottom of her shirt and splayed across the skin of her back, she felt no panic.

"You are so beautiful," he whispered as his mouth blazed a trail down the length of her neck. "From the moment I laid eyes on you, I wanted you."

She could feel his desire for her in the heat of his gaze, in the beat of his heart against hers and in the arousal that was made evident by the closeness of their bodies. Even that didn't cause any panic to rise up inside her. She felt in control, fired by the desire for him and the need to be okay with this.

His mouth found hers again and without breaking their kiss he guided her to the bed and they tumbled onto the mattress, arms and legs tangled together.

Still no thrum of panic filled her. It was going to be all right. She was going to be all right, she thought. And then he rolled them so he was half on top of her.

Suddenly things weren't all right. The scent of the jungle filled her head. She squeezed her eyes tightly closed, willing away the odor, the horrid memories that tried to grab her by the throat.

She was here in her bedroom with Randall, not in the jungle with those men. Randall would never hurt her, he'd never take from her what wasn't his to take, what she didn't willingly give.

As the weight of his body increased, a deep tremble began inside her. It wasn't desire, it was the rising panic…the feeling that she couldn't breathe that portended a full-blown panic attack.

As his mouth once again left hers and his hand moved to her stomach, she felt as if she were suffocating. Despair welled up inside her as she realized she couldn't fight it any longer.

"I can't." Her voice was half-hysterical as she pushed against him.

Instantly he rolled off her and sat up. Caitlin remained lying on her back, her eyes tightly closed as she listened to the sound of his rapid breathing.

"I'm sorry," she finally said, She refused to open her eyes. She didn't want to look at him, didn't want to see the expression of disgust that surely rode his features. "I thought I could do this. I wanted to do this, but I just can't stand the weight of your body on mine."

"You want to talk about it?"

Tears burned behind her eyelids. *Tell your father his old friends say hello.* The memories cascaded through her. "There's nothing to talk about," she finally replied. "It's just the way I am."

She felt his gaze on her, but she refused to look at

him. She was devastated, ashamed of her lack of control over her own emotions, and she felt once again as if she were nothing more than a shell of a woman...a dead woman.

"Caitlin, it's okay," Randall said softly.

"No, it's not okay." She finally opened her eyes and sat up. She wrapped her arms around herself, seeking some source of warmth. "I wanted you, Randall, but there's something wrong inside me. I feel trapped when I'm weighed down."

A small smile curved his lips. "There are other ways to accomplish the goal. I mean, I don't have to touch you. I don't have to be on top."

She shook her head, afraid to try again only to be further humiliated. "I think maybe I just want to go to sleep."

He nodded and started to stand, but she realized she didn't want him to go. "Randall, I know it's a lot to ask, but would you sleep in here with me?"

"No problem," he agreed easily. "Caitlin, I'm here to give you as much or as little as you need."

She stared at him for a long moment. In another life, in another time, she could have fallen in love with a man like Randall Kane. But she was stuck in this life at this time, a wounded woman half-crazy about a cowboy who had vowed never to love again.

Chapter 8

It had to be close to midnight, but Caitlin wasn't asleep and she knew Randall wasn't, either. Her nightgown felt hot, cumbersome, but she knew it was because of his nearness in the bed.

He was clad only in a pair of boxer shorts and he looked as hot almost naked as he did in his tight jeans and T-shirt. Although he wasn't touching her, she felt his presence as acutely as if he were right next to her, his skin against hers, his mouth against her ear.

She wanted him. Even with the debacle that had taken place earlier, she still wanted him. Her desire was what kept her awake, what made her nightgown feel oppressive and presented a deep ache inside her heart.

She rolled over on her side to face him. In the brilliant moonlight that drifted through the window she could easily see his face. He was so handsome, each of his features radiating strength of character. He'd suffered the worst that a man could—the loss of his wife—and she knew now it had been that tragedy that had sent him to the bottom of a bottle.

But he'd pulled himself out. He'd chosen to live. And she wanted to do the same thing. She didn't want just to exist, she wanted to live…and she wanted to love.

His eyes were closed but a muscle knotted in his jaw, confirming that he hadn't found sleep yet. The tops of his bare shoulders were visible where the sheet had fallen down. His skin beckoned her for a caress; the very scent of him made her want to burrow her face against the crook of his neck.

I don't have to be on top. His words were a titillating refrain in her head. *I don't have to touch you. I don't have to be on top.*

If she was the one in control would it make a difference? Her heart stepped up its rhythm at the very possibility. Was she not completely broken, but only needing some extra love and care?

Since that horrifying night in the jungle she'd felt as if she'd lost all control in her life, that somehow she wasn't making any decisions, but rather all the decisions were being made for her. Those men had taken her control away from her.

She needed to take back control, wanted to do it now, with him. She felt that if she didn't do something now, she might never be able to reclaim herself as a person, as a fully functioning woman.

I don't have to be on top. The words held such possibility and she realized she trusted him to understand if everything went bad again. She'd never know if it was possible if she didn't at least try. And the reward if it went right would be priceless.

Tentatively she reached beneath the sheet and placed her hand on his flat, hard abdomen. Instantly she felt his muscles tighten, but his eyes remained closed.

His skin was warm, inviting to the touch, and the fact that he remained completely impassive emboldened her further. She curled closer to him, her hand moving up his chest in a slow, languid caress. She felt him catch his breath and thrilled at his obvious response to her touch.

She raised up and leaned over him, and his eyes opened as she pressed her lips to his. He didn't touch her, but his kiss held enough fire to make her feel as if she'd been thoroughly caressed.

His heartbeat thundered against her palm for a moment and then she moved her hand back down his abdomen and stopped at the waistband of his boxers, a tremor of uncertainty sweeping through her.

"You're in control, Caitlin," he said softly. "Whatever you want, whatever you need, it's your move. You can stop whenever you want to and I won't be upset."

She paused, waiting for her throat to close off, for the scent of the jungle to fill her head and for panic to waft through her, but there was only the clean male scent of Randall and the sweeping desire not to stop what she was doing.

For the first time in weeks she felt wonderfully in control, alive with the passion that flowed through her veins. A sweet anticipation rose up inside her.

It was only when she plucked at his waistband that he finally moved, raising his hips just enough to help her take off the boxers. He rolled away from her and grabbed his wallet from the nightstand, then pulled out a condom and laid it out in easy reach.

Caitlin rose to her knees, her heart beating like thunder, and paused for a moment. Surely the room was dark enough that he wouldn't see the fading bruises on her ribs. And she wanted her nightgown off. Drawing a deep breath she pulled it over her head and threw it to the floor.

There was a tremble inside her, but it had nothing to do with fear, nothing to do with any rising panic.

It was need that shivered through her as she hesitantly ran her fingers across his thigh and then wrapped her hand around his rigid length. His eyes glowed in the moonlight, but he didn't move a muscle.

Her heart expanded as she began to stroke him, his hardness throbbing beneath her fingers. A deep shudder worked through him and she knew he was trying hard to maintain his control. The muscles on either side of his neck were taut cords that showed his inner battle.

Her own control was ebbing away as the white-hot need to be one with him filled her. She reached across him for the condom, her hands trembling clumsily as she tore the package and removed it.

His hands were clenched in the sheets at his sides as

she rolled the condom onto him. His eyes glittered like something wild in the night as she took off her panties and tossed them to the floor, leaving her naked as she straddled him.

As she eased down on him, she wanted to weep. No panic, no memories, no pain…there was just Randall and the sweet sensation of him buried inside her.

For several long moments she remained unmoving, just savoring the fact that she had succeeded. Randall released a small, strangled gasp and it was enough to make her want to move on him, with him.

Moving her hips against his, she heard another gasp of pleasure escape his lips and suddenly she wanted him to touch her, needed to feel his hands on her.

She grabbed his hands and guided them up to her bare breasts, reveling in the warmth as he cupped their fullness. It felt right and good. As his thumbs grazed across the tops of her turgid nipples, she shivered with delight.

Once again she thrust her hips with his, a rising tide of tension building inside her as he met her, thrust for thrust. She lost herself in the exquisite sensations that sang through her.

And then the tide that had been building…building swept over her. His release came at the same time and he gasped her name on a strangled cry as they both found sweet release.

She collapsed against his chest with a joyous burst of laughter. Proof of life. That's what she'd wanted and that's what this had been for her.

Proof that she was still capable of feeling good things, that she was still able to function as a loving, giving human being. Proof of life.

"I'll be right back," he whispered, and slid out of the bed and disappeared into the bathroom. She nodded in the darkness, too elated to speak.

A moment later he was back beside her and she curled up in his arms. "Hmm, I love the smell of your hair," he murmured softly.

She smiled. "Good shampoo."

"And I love the color of your hair," he replied.

"Good genes."

He laughed and this time there was no reminder of the laughter in the jungle. There was just Randall and the wonder of what they'd shared.

Within minutes he had fallen asleep, his breathing soft and even next to her.

Her heart filled with joy, with the knowledge that at least for this moment she was safe and sated. Never had she trusted a man as much as she trusted Randall Kane. And she desperately needed somebody to trust.

The only other man she'd trusted completely in her life was missing and could possibly be dead. Even if her father was alive he was mixed up in something terrible.

She shoved these thoughts aside, not wanting to think about anything bad at the moment. She snuggled closer against Randall and closed her eyes. It was late. She could think about all the bad things in her life in the morning. Tonight she just wanted to enjoy sleeping in Randall's arms.

* * *

The arms came out of nowhere and grabbed her tightly as the point of a knife pricked the side of her neck. "Make a sound and I'll slit your throat," he said as he dragged her away from the campsite.

The scream that begged to be released remained inside her as she found herself hauled deeper into the jungle where four other men awaited. The man with the knife threw her to the ground, and the others laughed and called her names. Several of them kicked her, the pain slicing through her ribs and stealing her breath.

Her heart beat frantically as they grabbed her arms, her legs, and pinned her down. The man who was obviously in charge leered down at her. "You are a beautiful woman," he said. "You excite me."

When he began to unbuckle his belt she knew what was going to happen, and as the scream finally made it to her lips it was stuffed back by a grimy hand that clamped tight against her mouth.

Trapped. She was trapped, and terror forced bile to surge up in her throat. Help me! For God's sake somebody please help me!

"Caitlin!"

Oh, God, how did they know her name? They shouldn't know her name! She shouldn't have been so careless. Why were they doing this to her?

"Caitlin, honey, wake up. You're having a nightmare."

The strong, deep voice sliced through the terror and

slowly the familiar vision of the jungle faded away. She opened her eyes and saw Randall's face. For one long agonizing moment she simply stared at him and then she launched herself into his arms.

"It's okay, it was just a bad dream," he said as she burrowed closer to him. His hands moved up and down her back, soothing strokes that she wanted to go on forever.

She couldn't speak. The residual horror of the nightmare, of the memory shook through her as his caresses on her back stopped and he tightened his arms around her. She didn't find his embrace oppressive, but rather comforting.

"Baby, you're okay. You're safe," he said.

Slowly the horror began to pass and her heartbeat returned to a more normal rhythm. Although Randall asked nothing, she felt the questions she knew he must have.

How could he not have questions after everything they'd been through, after knowing what little he did about her? He wouldn't be normal if he didn't have questions. And she owed him answers. He deserved to know the truth.

"It wasn't just a nightmare," she finally said. "It was a memory…a horrible memory."

She moved out of his embrace and sat on the edge of the bed, her back to him as she stared at the patterns of moonlight dancing on the wall in front of her.

She hadn't intended ever to tell anyone what had happened to her, but now she realized she had to tell

Randall. "You asked me what brought me home from my work." Although she felt strong and sure of what she was about to do, she was vaguely surprised that her voice trembled.

She drew a deep breath. "I was raped. That's what brought me home."

Rhett had suspected something like this, but hearing the stark words come from her crashed a killing weight onto his heart. It all made sense now: her desire to be in control, her need for him to be submissive and the darkness he'd sensed in her.

Sorrow and rage rose up inside him and he shoved both emotions away, knowing she didn't need either from him at this moment. He wasn't sure exactly what she needed, but he intended to try to give it to her.

Although he wanted to smash something, find the person responsible for hurting her and tear his head off, his immediate need was to be whatever she needed him to be right now. His sense was that, more than anything, what she needed was to be held by him.

He pulled her into his arms and they tumbled back on the bed where he cuddled her. She released a tremulous sigh and relaxed against him.

They didn't speak. He had no words for her and she didn't appear to want to talk at the moment. She just needed the connection of his arms around her making her feel safe, and the quietness to calm whatever storm raged inside her. He stroked her hair, the silky strands curling to cling around his fingers as if they, too, needed connection with a warm human being.

Being a man, it was impossible for him to completely relate to what she'd gone through, but he could definitely identify with the terror of being helpless, the unadulterated fear of being killed.

As a former cop he knew the taste of terror, the kind of fear that could close off your throat and make your knees buckle.

His mind flashed back to his years as a cop on the Detroit police force. Detroit was a tough town and there had been more than one time that Rhett had found himself in a situation where he was in fear for his life.

But he'd signed on for that when he joined the force. Caitlin hadn't signed on to be raped when she'd donated her time and skill to help others.

He tightened his arms around her and once again fought an anger he'd only felt once before—on the day that Rebecca had died in his arms. That day he'd been angry with fate. At this moment his anger burned for one man, the man who had hurt Caitlin.

"Why don't we go down to the kitchen? I think maybe I'd like some coffee," she said as she stirred against him. "And then I want to tell you exactly what happened."

He released her and got out of the bed. He was glad she wanted to go downstairs. He didn't want to hear the details from her in this intimate setting where they had made such beautiful love.

They both got out of the bed and while he put on his

jeans she grabbed her nightgown and pulled it over her head and then pulled a robe around herself, as well.

He held out his hand to her and she grasped it as if it were a lifeline as they walked down the stairs side by side.

When they reached the kitchen she sat at the table and he made a short pot of coffee. They didn't speak until the coffee had finished brewing and he'd poured them each a cup and joined her at the table.

Her pale, taut features once again forced emotion into his chest. He watched as she wrapped her fingers around the mug, as if seeking whatever warmth she could find.

"Tell me what happened whenever you're ready," he said, even though he suspected the details would simply feed the rage and grief bubbling inside him.

She nodded and took a sip of her coffee. "It had been a rough day," she said as she set the cup back on the table. "Too many people needing help, not enough supplies to do what needed to be done. It was frustrating every day, but this one had been worse than usual. By the time nightfall came I was discouraged and just wanted a little alone time." She paused and took another sip of her coffee, her gaze shooting off to the side of him.

He waited patiently, knowing the effort it was taking her to tell him what had happened to her. And in the moment of silence that ensued he recognized that she wasn't the only one who was going to be hurt when the truth came out about who he was and why he was here.

He wasn't going to leave here with his heart uninvolved and unscathed.

She set her cup back on the table and released a deep sigh. "Our campsite was in the middle of the jungle. We had plenty of armed guards but we'd been warned that the jungle was filled not only with wild animals, but also with marauding bands of men. We were in the middle of an area that was known for ruthless dope dealers and thieves. I never felt unsafe, but that night I guess I got too close to the perimeter of the camp and a man grabbed me."

Her throat worked convulsively, as if she had trouble swallowing, and when she looked at him again her gray eyes were nearly black. "He held a knife to my throat and told me if I screamed he'd kill me. He dragged me deeper into the jungle to where there were four men waiting."

Rhett's stomach twisted as he thought of her helpless and afraid at the hands of not one, not two, but five men. His face must have shown something for she leaned forward and held his gaze with hers.

"Only one raped me. The others held me down." Her cheeks flushed a vivid red and he had his answer about why she hadn't wanted him on top of her in a position of dominance.

She stared out the nearby window into the darkness of the night. Rhett waited patiently. There was no way he intended to prompt or hurry her. He knew she would tell him what she wanted to in her own time.

She released a deep sigh, still staring out the window.

"They threw me to the ground and kicked me in the ribs a couple of times. I didn't know what they wanted. I had no purse or anything with me so I knew it wasn't a robbery. The one who raped me…he seemed to be the leader of the group. The others did what he told them to do."

"Did they call him by name?"

She looked at him in surprise, as if she hadn't thought about it before. Closing her eyes, she grew very still and he could only imagine the images flashing through her head as she went back to the jungle.

Her eyes flung open. "Mark. One of them called him Mark." She leaned back in the chair, her skin returning to a more normal shade. "What difference does it make if I know his name or not?"

"I like knowing what name to curse," he replied, surprised to hear a tremble of emotion in his own voice.

To his further surprise she offered him a small smile. "I like the way you think."

He was grateful she couldn't know his thoughts, for they were definitely dark and ugly at the moment. "Did you report it to anyone?"

She shook her head. "I didn't tell anyone. I didn't want anyone to know. I felt dirty…ugly and so violated. When the men from my camp arrived I told them the men had tried to rob me. I didn't want to talk about it to anyone else. I didn't even want to think about it."

Rhett had been a cop long enough to know that it was common for the crime of rape not to be reported by women for a variety of reasons, and even though he wished Caitlin had reported it, he wasn't about to judge her for not doing so.

"Have you told Esme?"

"Definitely not," she replied quickly. "It would break her heart. Besides, what's important is that I survived," she said, pulling him from the dark place in his mind. "A little broken, a little battered, but I'm here and I'm going to be fine."

"You are some kind of woman." Admiration laced his voice. "You survived the jungle, Caitlin. I can't pretend to know how horrible it was for you, and when I think about it I want to smash Mark, whoever the hell he is, in the face so many times he needs a feeding tube to eat and a breathing tube to live."

Her smile fell and she leaned forward once again. "I think he meant to have me killed."

"Why do you say that?" It was Rhett's experience that most rapists weren't murderers. They were usually two different kinds of animals altogether.

Her eyes darkened once again. "When he finished, he gestured to one of the other men and made a throat-slashing gesture, but before the man could do anything one of the doctors and several guards came running and my attackers ran away."

Rhett hadn't touched her since she'd started her story, but he needed to now. He reached across the table and touched the back of her cold hand. She turned her hand over to accept his and squeezed tightly, as if he were a lifeline for her.

"I'm sorry, Caitlin," he said fervently and squeezed

her hand. "I'm so damned sorry. I wish I could go back in time and make things right. I wish I could go back in time and save you before anything bad could happen to you."

Once again a smile curved her lips and the darkness in her eyes lightened. "I think you have saved me, Randall. A week ago I wasn't sure I would ever trust a man again and yet I trust you. Two hours ago I didn't think I would ever make love again, but now I know I'm capable of that, as well."

Every word she said only made him feel worse. They were like daggers in his heart. Duty battled with emotion. What he wanted was to hear his real name fall from her lips if they made love again. He wanted to warn her not to get emotionally entangled with him because as soon as her father showed up, Rhett was going to arrest him and take him away.

But he couldn't think about all that right now. At this moment she needed nothing but support from him. "Your strength amazes me, Caitlin. No matter how things eventually play out between us I want you to know that I think you're not only beautiful, but strong and courageous, as well."

She released her hold on his hand and once again sat back in her chair, her forehead furrowed with a frown. "I'm not. I'm not courageous and strong at all. My time in the jungle has left me with nightmares and panic attacks. I could live with those, but now I'm afraid that my father might be dead."

Rhett straightened in his chair. "Why on earth would you think that?"

She got up from the table and carried her coffee cup to the sink and then turned back to face him. "I can't think of any other thing that would keep him from calling here. I think Esme has the same fear."

"That doesn't mean he's dead," Rhett protested. "You said he doesn't have any enemies and you haven't mentioned that he's sick or anything like that."

She shook her head. "No, he isn't sick." Her gaze slid from his and stared at a point just over his head. "As far as him having enemies, a daughter doesn't always know everything about her father."

There was something in her tone of voice that made Rhett wonder if she was telling the truth about her father's enemies, but he knew now wasn't time to confront her. Still, he had a feeling she knew more than she was saying.

His stomach twisted as he once again thought of her in the jungle, fearing for her life as she was raped by a man Rhett would like to hunt down and kill.

"I think I'm ready to go back to sleep," she said and released a weary sigh.

He realized the effort it had cost her to tell him what had happened to her, to go back to that place and time and relive the horror. Both physically and emotionally she had to be spent.

He got up from the table and carried his cup to the sink and then pulled her into his arms. She came willingly and laid her head against his chest.

Smelling the clean, fresh scent of her hair, a surge of protectiveness rose inside him. He never wanted her hurt again. She'd suffered so much already and it broke his heart that he knew the suffering wasn't done yet, that more damage would be done. Not by a stranger in a jungle but by him.

"Things will look better tomorrow," he said although he knew they were nothing but empty words.

He couldn't go back and fix what had happened to her, but he damned sure would do whatever it took to keep her safe from whoever had tried to kill her. He'd keep her safe and care for her until the moment he had to destroy her.

Chapter 9

Hank Kelley had hoped that things would look better with the dawn of a new day, but he was already having a bad day and it was only a little past nine in the morning.

He hadn't heard from Lana's kidnappers since he'd demanded proof of life from them, and the silence was positively terrifying.

They had initially sent him a videotape that had shown Lana alive, then there had been an interrupted phone call, but he'd seen nothing from them since he'd demanded new proof of life.

He had no idea where his wife was, and he wished he could talk to her. Sarah had gone into hiding when the mistresses had started coming forward. Hank supposed what they said was true, you didn't know what you had until it was gone.

Sarah had been the perfect political wife, supportive and beautiful. She'd ridden the campaign trail with him whenever possible, but once he'd been voted in as senator she had chosen to spend most of her time staying at home and being a good mother to their growing brood of children. He had thrown it all away with mistresses who, at the end of the day, had meant nothing to him. He'd been a stupid fool.

He entertained some crazy hope that if he made it out of this alive, if Lana came home safe and sound, somehow he'd be able to save the marriage he'd thrown away. Somewhere in the back of his mind he knew it was nothing more than a foolish man's regret. He doubted that he'd ever have his family back again.

During his time in self-imposed isolation here at the ranch he'd had a lot of time to think about his life and the direction it had gone. He'd never doubted that he was destined for greatness, and certainly, marrying Sarah had helped.

Sarah Mistler had been the wealthiest heiress in the United States when Hank had married her. He'd loved her, but there was no question he'd also known that she could help him achieve his goals. God, he wished she were here now. Sarah was smart and savvy and she'd help him figure out what to do.

At least one good thing had come out of this entire debacle. Hank and his half brother, Donald, had managed to reconnect. He and Donald had gone their separate ways years ago, torn apart by sibling rivalry and Hank's ambition.

Hank had been shocked when Donald had reached out to him and come to the ranch for a reunion. Donald's support after all these years had humbled him.

"Dad?" Cole appeared on the threshold of the guest room. "President Colton is here to see you." Cole's voice held surprise and also a touch of awe.

"Here? Now?" Hank stared at his son. He'd placed a call to Joe the day before, wanting to explain his position, needing the president to know that he, Hank, would never be part of a conspiracy to hurt him. Unfortunately, his conversation with the president had been brief.

"He's waiting for you," Cole said, breaking the inertia that had momentarily gripped Hank.

Hank followed his son down the hallway toward the great room, his heart pounding a million beats a minute. Maybe he was here to see Hank arrested, to throw him into a federal prison where the powerful members of the Raven's Head Society would see that he died.

Joe Colton had always been a man Hank admired. A family man with strong values and intelligence, Joe had united the country, except for a small group of men who wanted him dead.

God, what a tangled web Hank found himself in, and it seemed the more he struggled, the tighter the web squeezed around him. His mouth dried as he entered the great room where President Joe Colton awaited him.

Despite the fact that President Colton was in his early seventies, physically he was still an impressive man. Tall and fit, he was handsome, with bright blue eyes and salt-and-pepper hair that only added to his distinguished appearance. There was an aura of quiet power about him, a power that Hank had once envied.

"Hank," Joe said. As he held out a hand to greet Hank, Hank was embarrassed to feel the sting of unexpected tears in his eyes.

Hank gripped the president's hand tightly. "What are you doing here?" he asked when the handshake ended.

"My wife and I are in the area for several days. I managed to sneak away from official duties for a couple of hours and thought it would be good if we could talk… alone." Joe's eyes were kind as he gazed at Hank.

"I'll just leave you two alone," Cole said. A moment later the two men were seated on the sofa, Hank on one end and the president on the other.

"Would you like something to drink?" Hank asked.

"No, thanks, I'm fine. I've heard about your daughter's plight and I just wanted to offer you my full support," Joe said.

Once again Hank felt the press of tears as he thought about his daughter. "I've asked the kidnappers for proof of life, but so far I haven't heard back from them. I had no idea what I was getting involved in and now I don't know what to do," Hank confessed. "I don't know how to fix this. The last thing I wanted was for my daughter to be in danger, for you to be in any danger."

"I've never doubted your loyalty to me," Joe replied smoothly. "One of the reasons I wanted to speak with you was to assure you that I'm safe. My security people are taking this threat very seriously and we're being careful. You should be focusing all your energy on getting your daughter back."

"When I met with the men in the Raven's Head Society, I had no idea what their true goals were, what they intended to do," Hank continued. "I just thought they were concerned businessmen wanting to help better the country."

Joe held up a hand. "I won't ask you for any information that might put your daughter's life at risk."

It was this quality that made Joe Colton one of the most popular, most beloved presidents in the history of the United States. He understood the meaning of family and core values, of goodness and fairness. It was also these qualities that had made him a target of the powerful and wealthy businessmen who comprised the Raven's Head Society.

For the next few minutes the two men talked about family, about love and about the mess Hank found himself in. Hank found solace in Joe's quiet, calm support. Ultimately, however, when the president left, flanked by Secret Servicemen, Hank was no closer to figuring out what he was going to do. Only one thing was certain. The longer the kidnappers were silent, the more he feared for his daughter's life.

Caitlin paced the length of the living room, feeling as if she was going to jump out of her skin. She'd awakened that morning with a dreadful worry heavy inside her chest. She was afraid that whoever was after her would eventually succeed. She was worried about her father and why they hadn't heard from him.

Two days had passed since she'd confessed to Randall the events in the jungle, two days that she'd been cooped up inside the house like a prisoner.

Randall was in the kitchen chatting to Esme as the older woman made lunch, and it worried Caitlin just a little bit that the sound of his low, deep voice not only comforted her but also filled her with a longing for more. Not just more sex from him, but more of him in every aspect.

And she knew that down that path was heartache. He'd made it clear to her that he'd had his shot at love and happiness and had no desire to go there again. He traveled light and alone through life and she'd be a fool not to remember that.

One of these days the wind would blow a certain direction and he'd be gone. She figured there were only two things keeping him here now. The first was desire and the second was that somebody was trying to kill her.

There was no question that his desire for her hadn't waned with their lovemaking. They had made love again the night before. He'd been tender and had once again had allowed her to take the lead. She'd felt a healing inside her, a sense of taking herself back.

She wasn't foolish enough to believe that she was over the trauma of the rape. She knew that would take time and perhaps eventually some therapy to work through. But for now she had other things on her mind, such as her father's absence and Randall's very real, very intimate presence.

She'd spent part of the morning trying to analyze her feelings for Randall. If she weren't in fear for her life, if he hadn't stepped up as a bodyguard and been so understanding about her physical aversions, would she still feel so close to him?

No matter how she twisted things around in her head, the answer came back yes. With each minute she spent in his company she found more and more things about him that she liked, things about him that she admired.

Despite his rough-and-tumble exterior, in spite of the fact that she suspected he could have more than a little bit of a temper when faced with injustice, he also had a streak of tenderness that knew no bounds.

Caitlin wasn't sure if she knew what real romantic love felt like. Even though she was thirty-four, she was certain she'd never known that kind of love before.

All the men she had dated had been pleasant diversions, but she'd never felt that her heart had been invested in those men.

Randall gave her crazy butterflies in the pit of her stomach, he could weaken her knees with a single heated gaze, but that could be nothing more than lust.

He made her laugh and that was almost as sexy as the glint in his green eyes. He possessed a kindness that spoke of a good and true heart. Even if things weren't so complicated in her life at the moment she had a feeling she'd find Randall Kane more than desirable on every level. She'd definitely never felt like this about any man.

At that moment he walked out of the kitchen and into the living room where she was tearing up the floor with her pacing back and forth.

"What's wrong with you?" he asked. "You've been tense and on edge since you got up this morning."

She flung herself into a nearby chair and stared up at him. Dressed in a pair of jeans and a black T-shirt, with his hair unusually tousled and a five-o'clock shadow dusting his jaw, the man made the word *hot* seem ineffectual.

"I'm going stir-crazy," she said. "I feel like a prisoner who doesn't get any yard time."

He smiled sympathetically. "Most prisoners don't want yard time if they know it could be dangerous."

"I know." She sighed in frustration. "I know I shouldn't go out, but I'm going more than a little bit insane."

"Maybe after lunch we could do something that will take your mind off things." His eyes glittered in that way that made her know he was going to say something outrageous. "A couple of hands of strip poker might be entertaining."

She laughed. "Esme would have a heart attack if we did that at her kitchen table."

"Then we'll invite her to play, too," he replied easily, making her laugh again. "And we could always play in the dining room instead of in the kitchen if you have a problem with the setting."

The bad mood that had tried to take hold of her disappeared. "Maybe we'll play a few hands at the kitchen table but we'll keep our clothes on and I'll take you for your pocket change instead."

He pretended a scowl that did nothing to detract from his bad-boy handsomeness. "You women always want to ruin a man's attempt to have fun."

At that moment Esme called them into the kitchen for lunch. The meal passed with mundane conversation—the streak of good weather they were having, the Thanksgiving holiday approaching at the end of the month and the repairs that he had noticed needed to be done to the fence in one of the pastures.

After lunch Caitlin and Randall played poker while Esme decided to drive into town for some necessary groceries. Randall insisted she take Clint with her, not wanting Esmeralda to be out on her own.

Caitlin had a feeling Randall was keeping her busy with both the ordinary conversation over lunch and the card games so she wouldn't have a chance to think about what had happened...what could still happen.

Randall was an expert at bluffing and won every hand he and Caitlin played. And he was a horrible winner—bragging, with his dimples dancing and his eyes sparkling.

After the seventh game Caitlin threw her cards on the table in frustration. "Okay, I give up. I hate to admit it, but you're too good."

He grinned and began to gather up the cards. "If we'd been playing strip poker I would have had you naked by now."

"Not necessarily. I would have played harder, smarter with those kinds of stakes," she replied easily.

At the moment, with him smiling at her from across the table, with the laughter they had shared as they'd played cards, she felt so close to him it scared her more than just a little bit.

"Tell me about your wife," she said and somewhere in the back of her mind she knew that the subject would create a distance between them, a distance she desperately needed at the moment.

"What do you want to know about her?" His voice remained steady although his eyes darkened slightly in hue.

"What kind of woman was she? What did she like to do?" She wanted to know what kind of woman had captured his heart so completely that he would never want another woman in his life again.

He straightened the cards and then set the deck on the table and leaned back in his chair. "Her family moved to my hometown when we were both sophomores in high school. The minute I saw her I knew she was going to be mine. She was cute and blonde and had soulful brown eyes. She was bright and funny and to my complete surprise was as crazy about me as I was about her."

There was a softness to his features as he spoke, a softness that shot a wistfulness through Caitlin. No man had ever felt that way about her and she wanted that. She wanted a man's eyes to light with love for her, a man's voice to speak her very name with love.

Funny thing was, she knew that if she closed her

eyes and tried to imagine that man, he would be Randall Kane.

"She was a kind woman," he continued. "And she made me want to be a better man. She was going to school to become a social worker, but she also loved being a rancher's wife and we spent a lot of time together caring for the livestock."

"Do you ever think about owning your own ranch again?" Caitlin asked.

He hesitated a long moment before answering. "Never," he said with what appeared to be a forced firmness.

"That's too bad. You're so good with the horses, you could probably be very successful if you owned your own place."

"What about you? What do you see for yourself in the future?" he asked and she suspected he was intentionally turning the conversation away from himself.

"My plan was always to eventually open a private practice and own a ranch somewhere near here. I can't imagine urban living. I always wanted to be where I could have horses."

"Why haven't you already done that?"

She frowned thoughtfully. "When I was going through medical school, it was just easier to live here. I didn't have to worry about cooking or cleaning. All I had to do was focus on getting good grades. Living here seemed to be the smart thing to do at that time. That's the easy answer."

"And what's the complicated answer?" he asked.

"My father." As always, thoughts of Mickey shot a stab of worry through her. "I worried about him being all alone if I moved out. I couldn't stand the thought of him being lonesome."

She offered him a small smile. "Ridiculous, I know. But now that I have learned he has Esme, that he's always had Esme as more than just his housekeeper, it will make it easier for me to make my own life someplace else."

"And I suppose you're the white-fence-and-children kind of woman?"

It was her turn to hesitate a beat before answering, her heart constricting a little. "I was before El Salvador. I wanted it all—the practice, the husband and a couple of kids. Since then that particular dream hasn't really seemed possible."

"You'll have that dream, Caitlin...the private practice, the picket fence, the man who loves you and all the children you want. You're going to be fine, Caitlin." His voice had the same soothing quality that he'd used with Molly.

"Right, all I have to do is figure out where my father is and dodge the bullets of somebody who is trying to kill me. Other than that everything is going to be just fine." She waited for him to tell her once again that everything was going to be fine and when he remained silent the worry that she'd fought against since waking that morning raised its ugly head and filled her with a horrible sense of foreboding.

At that moment Esme returned, with Clint just behind

her carrying in bags of groceries. "Clint, how are things going?" she asked the tall cowboy as he placed several bags on the kitchen counter.

"Everything is going just fine, nothing for you to worry about. All the horses are in good shape. The addition of the oat hay in their diet is definitely making a difference."

"What about Molly?" she asked.

"I believe she misses Randall," he replied with an easy smile.

"What makes you think that?" Randall asked.

"Every time I step outside she raises her head like she's expecting somebody in particular and when she sees it's me she turns her back and faces the opposite direction." Clint offered them a wry grin. "Typical woman, why cozy up to the number-two man when you really want the number-one man."

Rhett smiled and Caitlin could see that he was pleased at the idea of the horse missing him. "Maybe I'll try to get outside this afternoon and spend a little time at the small corral," Randall said.

"I wouldn't mind getting outside for a little while myself," Caitlin said.

"That's not going to happen," Randall said firmly.

"Amen," Esme murmured under her breath.

Within minutes Clint was gone and Randall and Caitlin remained in the kitchen at the table. "Need some help?" Randall offered Esmeralda as she bustled to empty the grocery bags.

"She never wants help when she's putting away groceries," Caitlin said.

"I like things my own way," Esme agreed. "I consider this my kitchen and I have a certain way of doing things, specific places where things belong."

"Ah, a woman who knows exactly what she likes," Randall teased.

"That's right, and nobody gets into my pantry except me." Esme exclaimed as she carried two of the plastic bags into the small room.

"She talks a good game, but she's always been a pushover," Caitlin said in amusement.

Randall raised one of his eyebrows. "I'll bet between your father and her you managed to get away with murder."

She grinned at him. "Actually, I think if you were to ask both my father and Esme, they'd tell you that I was a pretty good kid who didn't need much discipline. Unlike you, from the stories you've told me about your childhood."

"I'll admit, I could be a little bit of a hell-raiser as a kid. My father was always threatening to take me out to the woodshed. Fortunately we didn't have a woodshed."

"And what about your mother? What did she threaten you with?" Caitlin loved hearing him talk about his past, the glimpses it gave her into the man he'd become.

He grinned. "She wanted to pin me up by my ears to the clothesline more than a few times. The idea of me hanging next to a pair of her white panties on the line scared me a lot more than the threat of the woodshed."

Caitlin laughed. "I can only remember one time when my dad really got angry with me. I was about twelve and had ridden a horse too hard and hadn't cooled her down before taking her back to the stables. When Dad found out he threatened to send me to boarding school where I wouldn't have a chance to abuse a poor innocent horse. I was horrified that I'd abused the horse and even more terrified of being sent away from here."

At that moment the phone rang. Esme was still in the pantry and so Caitlin jumped up to answer.

"Caty girl, what are you doing home?"

As she heard the deep, familiar voice of her father, the laughter she and Rhett had just shared vanished and Caitlin burst into tears.

Chapter 10

Rhett stepped out of the kitchen to give Caitlin some privacy, but he didn't go too far. He remained just outside the kitchen doorway where he could hear Caitlin's side of the conversation with her father.

Finally. Finally contact had been made and Rhett had no doubt that it wouldn't be long now before Mickey showed up here. He should feel elated that his time here was nearly done, that his job was nearly finished, but he didn't. He felt sick and sorry and dreaded what was to come.

"You have to come home." Caitlin's voice was thick with emotion. "I need you here, Dad. Something awful has happened, bad things are still happening and we need to talk."

Rhett had no idea what Mickey replied, but Caitlin's

next words shot pain through his heart. "I was attacked, Dad," she cried. "I was assaulted in the jungle and the man who assaulted me told me to tell my father his old friends said hello."

Rhett's heartbeat seemed to stop. What? She hadn't told him that. She hadn't mentioned that the rapist had said something about her father.

Had the words been said generally, the man knowing that the rape of a daughter would be any normal father's nightmare? Or was the man specifically talking about Mickey? And if that was the case, what was the tie between Mickey O'Donahue and a band of renegades in an El Salvadoran jungle?

"Where are you?" she asked. There was a moment's pause. "Just come home," Caitlin exclaimed. "Yes, okay. I'll see you then."

The call ended and he heard Esme sobbing hysterically. He could only imagine how Esme must be feeling to learn in this way that the child she had raised, the woman she loved as a daughter had been attacked, probably.

There was tearful conversation and when there was nothing more other than silence, Rhett stepped back into the kitchen. Caitlin stood in Esme's embrace, her cheeks reddened by her tears and her eyes holding a weariness of spirit that broke his heart.

"Those animals," Esmeralda said, her voice thick with anger, with grief. She released a string of Spanish curses. "I would kill those men if they were here in front of me." She patted Caitlin's back.

"I know," Rhett said. "And I'd be helping you kill them."

The grim smile Esmeralda gave him was one of firm approval, as if they were two warriors fighting the same enemy to save a precious princess.

"Your father is coming home?" he asked.

Caitlin moved out of Esme's embrace and nodded her head. "He said he'd be home sometime tomorrow."

Rhett wanted to ask her if the man who had raped her had said anything else, but he didn't want her to know that he'd been listening to her conversation.

"Everything is going to be fine when Mickey gets home," Esme said firmly, as if there was no other alternative possible. "We'll heal from all this and life will soon get back to normal."

Of course, Rhett knew that wasn't true. Nothing was going to get back to normal when Mickey returned home. Rhett was going to rip Mickey away from the daughter who needed him and the woman who loved him. Sometimes his job stank, and this was definitely one of those times.

The rest of the afternoon passed with the hands of the clock moving agonizingly slow. Caitlin was quiet, withdrawn, and Rhett didn't attempt to break through the wall she'd put up.

He needed to get some distance. It was time to start the difficult task of emotionally removing himself from her. He would have liked just once to hear her whisper his name, his real name, while they made love. He would have liked to hang around here until she'd healed completely, but he couldn't do that to her.

Tomorrow his real name would be a curse on her lips, she would hate him like she'd never hated before. He'd gotten close to her under false pretenses, lied to her about who he was and what he was doing here.

What hadn't been a lie was his desire for her each time he took her into his arms. What hadn't been a lie was the depth of his feelings for her. But none of that would matter when tomorrow came.

He'd called his boss to let him know what was going on, then had called the contact number he had for a couple of agents who were holed up nearby waiting for a pickup, to let them know it would occur the next day.

He was told that nobody had been able to locate the whereabouts of Garrett Simms. It was unknown whether the man was still in the area or not, which kept him as a suspect in the shootings.

If Rhett couldn't discount him, then he had to consider that the man might have a score to settle with the O'Donahues. Still, only a coward would go after Caitlin, only a coward would shoot at an unsuspecting woman.

After a quiet dinner Esme cleared the dishes from the table and then retired to her room, leaving Rhett and Caitlin alone on the sofa in the living room.

"You've been quiet this evening," he said.

She offered him a tired smile. "I have a lot on my mind. At least I'm grateful to know my dad is okay. I was really starting to worry that something bad had happened to him."

"Did he say where he was?" Maybe the kindest thing would be to pick Mickey up now wherever he was and not allow him to come home at all, not take him here in front of Caitlin and Esmeralda.

But Rhett knew how badly Caitlin needed to see her father, needed to feel Mickey's arms around her, and he suspected his idea of picking Mickey up somewhere else wasn't so much to save Caitlin and Esmeralda from pain, but to lessen his own pain in this whole ordeal.

"No. I asked where he was, but he said it wasn't important, that all that was important was that he'd be home sometime tomorrow. The number he called from wasn't a number I recognized, but I think he said something about buying a new cell phone."

An untraceable throwaway, Rhett thought. Mickey hadn't been stupid enough to call from a phone that could be traced. He obviously knew he was in deep trouble and was doing everything he could to stay under the radar.

But he had to know he was taking an enormous risk in coming home. The fact that he was willing to take that risk spoke of his enormous love for his daughter.

"Did he say what time he planned to arrive here?"

She shook her head. "No, he just said he'd be home at some point tomorrow. And if you don't mind, I think I'm going to call it a night, too." She rose from the sofa and Rhett stood, as well. "You'll be up later?" she asked.

"Maybe it would be best if I stayed in the guest room," he said. "I mean, I doubt if your dad would appreciate me sleeping in your bed." Besides, it felt so wrong, to sleep beside her, to sink into her scent, the warmth of her, knowing that tomorrow he would betray her.

She smiled tiredly. "Dad knows I'm a big girl. Besides, he's going to love you, Randall, especially when I tell him how you've kept me safe from harm and how you've been here for me emotionally through everything."

Her words couldn't have hurt him more if she'd taken a stake and driven it through the center of his heart. "Good night, Caitlin," he said. She murmured a goodnight and then he watched with a heavy heart as she climbed the stairs to her bedroom.

Once she'd disappeared from his sight he blew a sigh of frustration and returned to the living room. Never had he dreaded a morning like he did now. Never had he considered that the luscious redhead he'd seen get out of her car the day she'd arrived home would get so deeply beneath his skin and into his heart.

Her smile filled him with warmth, her tears moved him to despair and her courage awed him. If he'd wanted to settle down with one woman again it would be with a woman like Caitlin.

Of course, that's the last thing he wanted, he reminded himself. He would never forget the all-consuming grief of losing Rebecca. The scars of that loss were still deep in his soul. He refused to consider loving that deeply again.

Too restless to sit still, he moved to the window and stared outside where shadows of dusk would soon deepen to night. Suddenly he needed to be out of the house. Besides, he wanted to check on Molly one last time before he left this place for good.

He stepped outside and carefully locked the door behind him and reengaged the security system. He had a key to get back inside and knew the security code and was confident Caitlin would be safe with the door locked and him at the small corral.

He took a deep breath of the cool night air and wondered how long it would take for his head to empty of Caitlin's sweet scent. How long would he miss the sound of her voice? The feel of her warm curves snuggled against him as he fell asleep?

She was the last thing he'd expected, the last thing he'd wanted in his life. He'd vowed after he'd lost Rebecca that he'd never care about anyone that deeply again. He'd never wanted to feel that kind of grief again, but Caitlin had found her way into his heart.

"Hey, girl," he said softly as he approached the corral. Molly's ears pricked up and to Rhett's surprise the horse took a couple of steps toward him and then stopped. No matter how much Rhett cajoled the horse refused to come any closer.

But those couple of steps Molly had taken in his direction warmed his heart. If he'd only had more time here he was confident he would have had Molly taking apple slices from his hand. He could have worked with her until she trusted humans again.

He walked over to the foreman's cabin and sat on

the small porch and his gaze went to the house, to the window of Caitlin's bedroom.

He knew now that like Molly, Caitlin had been traumatized and it was going to take time and a very special man for her to completely trust again.

You could be that man, a little voice whispered in his head. With enough time he could help Caitlin through the trauma she'd endured, help make her whole again. She was already making great strides to healing and there was a part of him that wished he could be here to see her whole and completely healthy again.

He hoped she would find a man who could love her the way she deserved to be loved, a man who would be patient and understanding. He wanted her to have her practice and her ranch. He wanted her to have the children he'd once wanted. Dammit, he wanted her happiness and, as he thought of the morning to come, his heart grew heavy.

He remained seated on the porch while night fell completely and the only illumination was a silvery cast of moonlight that gave the grounds a ghostly appearance.

His thoughts were troubled. For the first time since Rebecca's death he questioned the path he'd taken in life. There was no question that he'd drifted into his current occupation and there was no question that he'd loved the work he'd done here at the ranch.

He'd told Caitlin the truth when he'd said he'd never considered owning his own ranch again, but there had been a little piece inside him that had come alive with the thought.

It was getting late and he knew he should go back inside, but he was reluctant to go back into the house, to crawl into bed next to the woman who would hate him by this time tomorrow night.

Still, he couldn't stay out here all night. It was possible Mickey would show up quite early in the morning. He started to rise and then froze as something caught his attention at the side of the house.

A moving shadow?

A figment of his imagination?

His breathing went shallow as he reached down to grab his gun from his ankle holster. Had he seen somebody? He wasn't sure. Maybe it had been nothing more than a dancing shadow made from the night breeze that stirred the nearby trees, but whatever it was, he intended to investigate.

He moved silently, hugging the deeper shadows as he made his way toward the house. His heart began an unsteady rhythm as adrenaline flooded his system.

When he reached the front corner, he gripped his gun firmly with both hands and turned to gaze down the side of the house.

Nothing.

He lowered the gun and drew a deep breath as he advanced down the side wall of the house. When he reached the next corner he once again got a grip on his gun and took the corner.

The man was visible in the moonlight. He was

pouring gasoline on the side of the house and the odor of the gas burned Rhett's nose.

"Halt!" Rhett yelled.

The man's head snapped up. He threw the can aside and took off running in the opposite direction. Rhett muttered a curse. There was nothing more he'd like to do than shoot the man, but he knew that if he did he took the chance of killing him and not getting answers. And he desperately wanted to know who was after Caitlin and why.

Shoving his gun in his waistband, Rhett took off after the man. If he had to, he'd shoot, but he'd much rather catch him and if necessary beat the answers out of him. Still, there was no way Rhett intended to allow the man to evade capture. One way or the other, the man was his.

The man obviously wasn't a runner and had no endurance, and it didn't take long for Rhett to gain on him. The man's labored breathing was audible as Rhett pumped his legs, his lungs burning as he focused only on bringing the man down.

There was no question in his mind that this was the person who had shot at Caitlin, no question in his mind that the man's intention had been to start a fire either to kill them all or to flush Caitlin out of the house where he could take another shot at her.

This thought spurred him on, and when he was within reach he lunged, catching the man by the shoulders and bringing him down to the ground.

The dark-haired man didn't go down without a fight.

He rolled to his back and slammed Rhett's chin with a right cross that shot pain through Rhett's entire skull. He answered with a punch fueled by rage. Blood spurted from the man's nostrils as he cried out in pain.

He slammed Rhett in the stomach with a force that whooshed the breath from him. Rhett rolled away, his lungs aching as they tried without success to draw a breath.

Get up, a voice commanded. *Caitlin needs you. Get up and take control of the situation.* As the man struggled to his feet, obviously ready to run again, Rhett knew if he didn't move immediately the man would disappear into the night and no questions would ever be answered.

Still on the ground, Rhett used his foot to sweep the legs out from under the man. The man slammed back down to the ground and Rhett struggled to his feet with his gun in hand.

"Get up," he commanded.

"Don't shoot," the man cried with his hands raised defensively in front of his face.

"Get up," Rhett repeated. "And if you make a move I don't like, I'll pull the trigger without blinking an eye," he warned as he tried to control the rage that made him want to pound the man with his fists.

Rhett did a quick pat-down and pulled a gun from the man's pants. Was this the weapon that had fired the bullets at Caitlin? A new rage threatened to engulf him.

"Are you Garrett Simms?" he asked, cursing the fact

that he hadn't even gotten a physical description of the former foreman from anyone.

The man frowned. "I don't know this Simms person," he replied.

"Who in the hell are you and what are you doing here?"

The man raised his chin, his eyes glittering darkly. "I don't have to tell you anything."

Rhett shoved the extra gun into his waistband and then motioned the man back toward the corral. Once there he grabbed a length of rope lying on top of one of the fence posts and bound his hands behind him. One way or another Rhett was going to get some answers from this man, he thought grimly. At the moment he didn't care if he had to beat them out of him.

"You can either make this easy on yourself or you can make it hard," Rhett said as he tied the ropes tighter than necessary.

The man must have heard something in Rhett's tone of voice that unsettled him. "I was only following orders," the man exclaimed, with a thick Spanish accent. "You must protect me. I can't go back to El Salvador. If I return there I'm a dead man."

Rhett's blood froze. El Salvador? What in the hell was going on here? What was a man from El Salvador doing here on a California ranch?

Was this the man who had attacked Caitlin in the jungle? Once again a red veil of rage threatened to consume him. He fought against it, knowing that rage made mistakes.

There was only one way to know for sure if this man was one of Caitlin's attackers and he hated the fact that he thought he just might be bringing her nightmares out of the jungle and right into her home.

Caitlin was awakened by Randall touching her shoulder. She opened her eyes, leaving sweet dreams behind and blinked against the overhead light he'd apparently turned on when he'd entered the room.

"What's going on?" she asked drowsily.

"I need you to get dressed and come downstairs," he said. "I caught a man trying to set fire to the house."

She bolted up, alarm rushing through her as sleep fell away. "Who is he? Where is he now?"

"I've got him tied up downstairs and I don't know who he is, but I'm hoping you'll know him." His green eyes were hard, his mouth set in a grim slash as he stared at her intently. "Caitlin, I think he might be one of the men who attacked you in the jungle."

Her heart crashed against her ribs and she wanted nothing more than to burrow beneath her blankets and ignore what he'd just told her. But, at her core, that wasn't who she was and she drew a deep, steadying breath and got out of the bed.

"I'll meet you downstairs," Randall said as he left the room.

Caitlin quickly pulled on a pair of jeans and a T-shirt, her mind buzzing with thoughts. If Randall was right, why would one of those men follow her here to try to kill her? She had no idea who they were, would probably never run into them again, so it didn't make any sense.

Nothing in her life made sense at the moment, nothing except Randall. If the man downstairs was one of the men from the jungle, then she knew she hadn't just been a random victim. This meant her attackers had known her name. They'd known where she lived. This thought positively chilled her to the bones.

Once she was dressed she paused at the top of the stairs, her heart beating so fast she felt short of breath.

The faces of the men in the jungle were indelibly burned into her memory, facial features she knew would be there for the rest of her life. Her knees weakened at the thought of seeing one of those faces again.

She looked down the stairs and saw Randall at the bottom waiting for her. His eyes held a supportive glint and as he raised his hand toward her, she realized she was in love with him.

As she walked down the stairs her heart expanded in her chest with the realization of the depth of her feelings for him. She loved him. She wasn't sure exactly when it had happened, but there was no denying the fact.

She could face anything with Randall at her side. She wanted him by her side not just at this moment, but for the rest of her life.

But she knew wishing it wouldn't make it come true. He was a ranch hand who blew with the wind and she had seen no indication that he was going to be anything different than that.

Still, as she walked down the stairs and took his hand

with hers, she was grateful he was here with her now. "I've got him in the kitchen," he said.

As they walked through the living room Caitlin smelled the odor of the jungle and felt the familiar tremble inside her. Randall tightened his hand around hers, and she drew strength from his nearness and support.

She saw him from the back first. Randall had tied the man to a kitchen chair and all she could see as she approached were the man's big hands tied behind the chair and a headful of glossy black hair.

It wasn't until she stepped in front of him that she momentarily lost her breath as she was cast back to that night, to that time of terror. Even with the bloody nose she recognized him.

He was a vision from her nightmares, a living, breathing part of the worst experience she'd ever had in her life. She fought against the bitter taste in her mouth, against the rising panic that threatened to consume her.

"He's one of the men from the jungle," she finally said when she felt in complete control. "He wasn't the man who raped me but he helped to hold me down."

She sensed Randall's anger and held tightly to his hand, this time wanting to give him the strength to maintain control. "What's your name?" he asked the man.

"Juan. Juan Gonzales." He looked at Caitlin. "I was only following orders. I didn't want to hurt you. Please, you have to help me."

Since the rape, the men in the jungle had become bigger-than-life monsters in Caitlin's mind. Now, as she saw Juan's dirty jeans and paunchy belly, his smashed nose and small eyes, she felt liberated from her visions.

He wasn't an all-powerful monster, but rather just a man, a pathetic little man who had attacked a helpless woman. He was nothing and she would give him no more power.

"Why are you here? Why are you trying to hurt Caitlin?" Randall asked.

"I was sent here because she can identify *mi capitan.*" Juan's eyes turned sly. "He is a great man. He's coming to America and will be a powerful, important man and we'll all ride on his coattails and become wealthy men."

"Who is he? I want his name," Randall said.

Juan's eyes narrowed in obvious fear. "He will kill me if I tell you his name."

Randall released his hold on Caitlin's hand and took a step closer to Juan. "And I will kill you if you *don't* tell me his name. I'm here now with a gun and your boss is very far away."

There was no question in Caitlin's mind that Randall would follow through on his threat and she saw on Juan's face that he believed it, too.

"If I tell you his name, then you must see that I get put into protective custody. I want protection. He will kill me and if he doesn't kill me then somebody from the Raven's Head Society will kill me."

Caitlin gasped at the name of the secret society. "What do you have to do with the Raven's Head Society?"

"*Mi capitan,* he works for them. It was the society

who ordered that we frighten you as a message to your father. Unfortunately he got carried away and…" Juan shrugged his shoulders.

"What message to my father?" she asked.

"It was a warning to him, that the society can hurt him, can hurt the people he loves and he'd better keep his mouth shut. Now, I've told you what I know. You put me in protective custody, yes?"

"We need to call the police," Caitlin said.

"Already done," Randall replied and then he looked at Juan once again. "And now you'll tell me his name."

Juan held eye contact with Randall for a long moment, and then released a sigh. "Marc. Marc Jiminez."

Marc Jiminez. A small shudder worked through her. She now had the full name of her rapist. Caitlin's head ached with the chaos of her thoughts. More than anything she needed her father. She had to find out his connection to the Raven's Head Society.

"Why don't you go back upstairs and I'll take care of this," Randall said. "I'll tell the authorities that they can speak to you sometime tomorrow."

Caitlin gazed at him gratefully. Her brain was too fried to make a coherent statement tonight. All she wanted was to get away from the man in the chair and let Randall handle all the details.

Still, she remained rooted in place and stared at one of the faces that had haunted her dreams. Before she realized her intent, she slapped him hard across his cheek. Instantly her hand stung, but she was filled with righteousness.

"Now I'm ready to go upstairs," she said and with a nod to Randall she left the kitchen.

When she was in her room she got undressed and into her nightgown and then got back into the bed. Her thoughts filled with Juan and the Raven's Head Society and her father. She rolled over to Randall's side of the bed where the pillow retained his scent.

She loved him and there were moments when she believed he loved her, too. But perhaps that was only wishful thinking on her part. She wanted him to love her enough to stick around, to build a life with her. She wanted him to love her enough to ignore the wind when it blew in his ear.

Randall loving her would almost make up for all the bad things she'd been through. Unfortunately, she didn't think that was going to be the case. He'd made it clear over and over again that he was just here for the short term, that his heart was unavailable to any woman.

It was almost an hour later when Randall finally came into her bedroom. She was seated on the end of the bed, sleep impossible with everything that had happened. "Is he gone?"

He nodded. "They picked him up and said they'd be in touch." He sank down next to her and took her hand in his. "You okay?"

"Surprisingly, yes," she replied thoughtfully. "I feel as if seeing one of those men again somehow gave me back my power as a woman."

"That slap you gave him was an awesome thing to behold." Randall's eyes held a glittering light that she wished she could see for the rest of her life.

She frowned as she thought of the man. "But I'm so confused about what my father has to do with all this."

"The Raven's Head Society. What do you know about that?" he asked.

"Not enough," she admitted. "The first time I even heard about it was when I spoke to one of Senator Hank Kelley's sons a couple of days ago. He told me Hank and my father had somehow gotten themselves involved in this secret society that has plans to kill President Colton."

"Wow, heavy stuff," he replied.

"Yeah, well, I don't believe for a minute that my father would ever be involved in such a thing. He's always supported President Colton, and so has Hank." Her heart squeezed painfully tight. "Apparently somebody from the society kidnapped Lana, Hank's daughter. She's the friend I told you about who's in danger. Who are these people who would order men to kidnap a daughter and terrorize another to achieve their goals?"

The question was rhetorical. She knew Randall had no answers for her. She squeezed his hand. "Randall, I know you didn't sign up for all this and I'm sorry that you've become a part of it."

"Don't apologize." He dropped her hand and stood and walked to the window where he peered out into the night. "Juan admitted that he took those shots at you, so at least we've solved that part of the mystery." He turned back to look at her. "And I hope that tomorrow you'll get the answers you need from your father."

She sensed a distance in him, as if his mind was already a thousand miles away from this place and her. Could she blame him? He'd come here to do a job, to work on the ranch as paid help and instead had found himself embroiled in her personal issues, in a murder scheme. He was probably more than ready to get out of here, to find a job somewhere else where nothing was required of him except the feeding and care of animals.

She heard the wind blowing and it whispered through her with a sense of despair as she realized Randall would soon be gone.

Chapter 11

Today is the day you'll break Caitlin's heart. This was Rhett's first thought when he opened his eyes the next morning. Today was the day she'd learn his real identity and she would hate him.

She was now curled up against his side, the scent of her filling his head. Her body was warm, but did nothing to warm the cold dread inside him.

At this moment Rhett hated Mickey O'Donahue for getting involved with the Raven's Head Society, and he hated himself for the job he was about to complete.

In the first couple of days at the ranch, he'd remembered how much he loved working on the land, dealing with livestock. Being an FBI agent had never been part of his life plan, had never been something he dreamed of doing.

He'd loved ranching, but had given it all up after losing Rebecca. It was as if in his grief he'd felt the need to punish himself by giving up what he'd loved most.

There had been more than a little bit of magic here at the O'Donahue ranch, working with the animals once again, indulging in his attraction to Caitlin. But now the magic was gone and painful duty called.

Quietly, he rolled away from Caitlin and out of the bed. He padded into the guest room next door, grabbed clean clothes and then hit the shower.

He was glad they hadn't made love the night before. Somehow if they had he knew it would only make today worse. And it was going to be bad enough as it was.

She'd been healing, taking back her power as a strong human being but he had a feeling today was going to shatter her newfound strength.

Once he was dressed he checked in on Caitlin, who was still sleeping soundly, then he followed the scent of freshly brewed coffee and something cinnamon down the stairs.

Esmeralda was in the kitchen, humming beneath her breath as she checked on the cinnamon rolls baking in the oven. She smiled as Rhett came into the kitchen. "It's a good day," she exclaimed. "Mickey will be home and everything is going to be fine."

Rhett walked over to the counter and poured himself a cup of coffee and then carried it to the table and sat, looking at yet another woman he was going to betray.

"Mickey is just like Caitlin, they both love my cinnamon rolls so I got up extra early this morning and made a double batch." She straightened and wiped her hands on her apron. Her lips trembled slightly. "My poor Caitlin. When I think of what happened to her I want to cry. Thank God you've been here for her." She cast him a sly glance. "I see the way she looks at you. You have become very important to her."

Jeez, as if he wasn't already feeling bad. "She'll be fine. She's an amazing, strong woman."

"Even a strong woman needs somebody special in her life," Esmeralda countered.

Rhett didn't reply. Instead he sipped his coffee and wished he were any place else on earth while this day unfolded.

It didn't help that he was exhausted. He'd lied to Caitlin when he'd told her he'd handed Juan over to the local authorities.

Instead he'd called his fellow agents to pick him up. Juan would be grilled about what he knew about the Raven's Head Society, and Rhett knew that somebody would be dispatched to deal with Marc Jiminez. Rhett's personal hope was that the man didn't live to see another sunrise for what he'd done to Caitlin.

After Juan had been picked up, Rhett had crawled into bed with Caitlin at her insistence that she needed him close to her. He'd remained awake for a long time after she'd fallen asleep, hating himself and what he was about to do to her.

"How about some breakfast?" Esmeralda asked, pulling him from his dismal thoughts.

"Sure, if it's not too much trouble," he replied. Nothing worse than betrayal on an empty stomach.

"No trouble at all," she replied.

As she bustled around, placing bacon in a skillet and cracking eggs, Rhett directed his gaze out the window and wondered when Mickey would arrive home.

The man had given Caitlin no idea where he was holed up. For all Rhett knew it might take him the whole day to travel back home or he could appear at any moment.

Rhett had his fellow agents standing by and the only thing left to do was wait for the man to show up, wait for the real heartache to begin.

He was halfway through his breakfast when Caitlin walked into the kitchen. He couldn't remember her ever looking more beautiful. Her glorious hair was loose and fell in soft waves around her shoulders. Her eyes were bright and she looked eager for the day to unfold.

Instead of her usual jeans and a T-shirt, she was dressed in a pair of black dress slacks and a black-and-white blouse that looked both sexy and classy at the same time. The fact that she'd dressed up to see her father only served to make Rhett feel worse than dirt.

"Good morning," she greeted him and sat in the chair across from him. Impishly she plucked a piece of bacon from his plate. "Mmm, I'm starving this morning." She bit into the bacon and then flashed him a quick grin.

"Don't you eat off his plate like a silly child," Esmeralda scolded. "I'll have your breakfast ready in just a few minutes."

"It's going to be a great day," Caitlin said. "Dad will be home and we'll finally get to make sense of everything that's happened. Then we'll figure out what he needs to do to get himself out of the mess he's in."

Esmeralda placed a cup of coffee in front of Caitlin and then laid a hand on Rhett's shoulder. "And we'll tell Mickey how lucky we were when Randall showed up on the doorstep looking for a job."

Caitlin's eyes darkened for a moment. "And hopefully Randall isn't hearing the call of the wind just yet."

Esmeralda frowned and moved to the window. "Is the wind blowing this morning? I hadn't noticed."

"A little inside joke," Rhett replied, although he was the last one who felt like laughing. Caitlin and Esmeralda didn't know it yet but there was a virtual gale blowing that would take him away.

He was aware of Caitlin looking at him expectantly, as if willing him to tell her he wasn't going anywhere. Instead of answering her, he picked up his coffee and stared out the window. This was definitely going to be one of the worst days of his life.

After finishing his breakfast, he left Caitlin, who was still eating, and went outside, needing desperately to distance himself from both the women.

As usual he found himself at the small corral. Molly neighed as if in greeting but kept her distance. In all probability he'd be gone by nightfall, leaving devastation behind.

He'd be onto another assignment and would return to

his solitary life. It was the way he'd wanted it, the way he'd chosen to live, he reminded himself.

He hoped Clint or Caitlin would continue to work with Molly. He hoped eventually Caitlin would heal enough to love somebody. He felt as if he was leaving behind so many loose ends here.

Molly was on the verge of trusting him and with a little more time and work would heal, but he wouldn't be here to see it. And Caitlin…after today he'd never see her face again, never hear the sound of her laughter or know the pleasure of holding her in his arms.

He'd been told to get close to Caitlin and he'd achieved his goal, done his job far too well. It would be a long time before he could finally get her out of his heart.

He tensed as he gazed out in the distance and saw a puff of dirt that signaled the approach of a car. Already? The odds were good that it was Mickey returning home.

He headed back into the house, his heart heavy with dread. "A car is coming," he said to Esmeralda and Caitlin who were both still in the kitchen.

Caitlin jumped up out of her chair as Emeralda quickly washed her hands at the sink. Rhett followed Caitlin as she flew out the front door and stood poised on the porch.

Rhett's information about Mickey was that the man drove a BMW and the car that pulled to a halt in front of the house was an old beat-up Ford. Still, it was definitely Mickey O'Donahue who got out of the driver's door.

With a small cry Caitlin launched off the porch and

into her father's arms. As Rhett saw Mickey embrace her in a bear hug, his heart grew even heavier.

If he was going to do his job, right now would be the time he'd step in, identify himself and take Mickey into custody, but he couldn't do it—not yet. Caitlin needed time with her father and, duty or not, Rhett wasn't going to deprive her of that totally.

Mickey was just as Caitlin had described him. Although not a particularly tall man, he gave the aura of power and strength. His long, light auburn hair was tied at the nape of his neck and he wore a pair of jeans and a navy polo shirt that stretched across beefy shoulders and arms.

The two stood together for several long moments, talking to each other. They were too far away for Rhett to hear their words, but he knew that whatever was being said was important to both of them.

Finally they released each other and, as he and Caitlin approached the porch, Rhett noticed that Mickey's fair skin looked slightly sun-damaged, his nose was a bit crooked, but his eyes were keen and radiated intelligence as his gaze swept over Rhett.

"Dad, this is Randall Kane," Caitlin said when they reached him. "He's taken over for Garrett Simms as foreman and I don't know what I would have done without him over the last week."

Mickey grasped Rhett's hand in a firm, no-nonsense shake. "If that's the case then it's nice to meet you, Randall." He threw his arm around Caitlin's shoulder. "I'm glad somebody was here to take care of my little girl. Let's get inside where we can talk."

Rhett followed behind father and daughter as they entered the house. Mickey released Caitlin only long enough to greet Esmeralda. The two hugged for a long moment and exchanged whispers before Mickey finally released her.

Minutes later they were all seated in the living room. Rhett had thought he'd give Caitlin and her father a little alone time, but Caitlin captured his hand and pulled him down next to her on the sofa while Esmeralda and Mickey took the two chairs opposite them.

"You can speak freely in front of Randall," Caitlin said to Mickey. "He knows about what happened to me in the jungle and we know this has something to do with a secret society."

Mickey's features seemed to crumple in on themselves as he gazed at his daughter. "I would kill somebody for what they did to you," he said in a broken voice as he buried his face in his big hands.

"Dad, please tell me what's going on," Caitlin said. "Dylan Kelley told me that you and Hank got involved with a plot to kill the president."

Mickey shook his head, and when he pulled his hands from his face his features looked ravaged by guilt and more than a whisper of fear. "We didn't know. We didn't know what we were getting involved in. We thought it was just a group of wealthy, powerful businessmen getting together to figure how best to help the country through the tough times that have been going on. We didn't realize what their true goal was until we were in too deep and then we didn't know what to do. I thought if we just distanced ourselves, laid low for a little while it would all go away."

He shook his head and his gaze was soft as it lingered on Caitlin. "I thought you were safe from all this. I thought you were out of the country and nobody could harm you." Grief darkened his eyes, a father's grief for his daughter's pain.

"Apparently this Raven's Head Society has very long arms," Rhett said. "Caitlin was not only attacked in the jungle, but the man behind the attack sent somebody here to kill her."

"Randall caught him last night trying to set the house on fire. He told us he was sent here by a man named Marc Jiminez. Do you know this Marc?"

"No, but I didn't know a lot of what was going on with the society," Mickey replied.

"We turned the man who tried to set the fire over to the authorities," Caitlin said.

"Then I owe you more than I'll ever be able to repay you for keeping my loved ones as safe as possible," Mickey said to Rhett.

"Did you know Lana has been kidnapped?" Caitlin asked.

Mickey nodded. "I spoke to Hank this morning before coming back here. He's holed up at Cole and Dylan's ranch in Montana."

"So, what happens now?" Caitlin asked.

"I don't know. The members of the society would

like me dead and I'm sure the government would like me behind bars." Mickey leaned back in his chair and released a weary sigh.

He closed his eyes for a long moment and when he opened them again there was a fire blazing in the blue depths. "I owe the society no allegiance. I don't believe in their goals or their methods. After what they did to you, I'd like to see them all burn in hell. I've been afraid to come forward with the information I have knowing that by talking I'd put a target on my back, but after what was done to you, I'll gladly take the target to see these men shut down."

Rhett knew it was time to make his move. In waiting he was just prolonging the inevitable and suddenly he just wanted it over and done.

He stood and pulled his badge from his pocket. "Mickey, I'm FBI Special Agent Rhett Kane and I'm here to take you into custody." As he said the words he shot a quick glance to Caitlin and he knew if he lived to be a million years old he'd never forget the look on her face.

Caitlin felt the earth tilt beneath her as she stared at the man she'd thought she knew, the man she had grown to love. Had she suddenly lost her mind? Had she heard him wrong?

Mickey released a rusty laugh and rose to his feet. "Well, well, if this isn't a hell of a surprise."

Esme began to weep as Caitlin continued to stare at Randall…or Rhett…or whatever his name was. An FBI agent? The cowboy with the dusty boots and charming smile was an FBI agent? He was here because he wanted to arrest her father?

She felt removed from herself, as if her brain couldn't quite compute what was happening and her emotions were just out of reach.

"You gonna cuff me?" Mickey asked as he placed his hands behind his back.

"I don't think that's necessary, is it?" Rhett pulled his cell phone from his pocket, hit a number and held it to his ear. "Need a pickup," he said and then clicked off and dropped the phone back in his pocket.

"I'd already decided to turn myself in. You're just making it easy on me," Mickey said.

"If you cooperate I'm sure something can be worked out to get you back home as soon as possible," Rhett replied.

Empty promises, Caitlin thought, some of the numbness beginning to wear off. He couldn't know what her father might be facing.

He'd lied. The words thundered through her brain. From the moment he'd stepped on the front porch and wrangled a job out of Esme, everything had been lies.

Everything he'd done, everything he'd said to her had been a calculated move to stay close so he would be here when Mickey came home. Every touch they'd shared, every secret revealed and shared, everything had been a big, fat lie.

Anger began to bubble just beneath the surface, an anger she didn't fight but rather embraced. She began to shake, tears burning at her eyes, as her father walked over to her and embraced her.

"Don't be afraid, Caty girl," he said as she burrowed against him. The scent of cigars and his familiar cologne might have comforted her if her feeling of being utterly and totally betrayed wasn't resonating through her.

"Everything is going to be fine," Mickey said as he kissed her on the forehead and then released her. "We'll all get through this somehow."

She watched as he walked over to Esme and pulled her onto her feet and into his arms. He whispered to her for a moment, kissed her on the forehead and then let go of her. "I'll be home as soon as I can."

He then looked at Rhett. "Let's go outside and wait for whoever is coming for me."

For the first time since he'd stood and identified himself, Rhett looked at Caitlin. "I'll be back in. We need to talk."

"Don't bother," she replied through tight lips. She held his gaze defiantly, seeing in his regret, remorse and the guilt of a man who knew exactly what he had done.

She'd had less than twenty-four hours to savor the fact that she was in love with him, but she'd have a lifetime to regret loving him, to hate him for what he'd done.

As the two men walked out of the front door Caitlin felt as if her heart went with them. One man had earned her love through a lifetime of caring, the other had stolen her love under false pretenses.

She was empty, bereft in a way she'd never known before. She turned and Esme grabbed her in a tight embrace, the older woman weeping the tears that Caitlin couldn't release.

Once again a numbness had overtaken her as the depth of Rhett's betrayal sank in. Esme finally released her. "We must be strong," she said. "We must stay strong until your father comes home. And he will come home soon!" She said the words as if by her sheer willpower alone she could make them come true.

As she disappeared back into the kitchen, Caitlin sank down on the sofa. He'd held her in his arms. He'd kissed her and made love with her as if she'd meant something to him. He'd insinuated himself into her life, into her very heart, and all he'd been after was her father.

Looking back she now remembered how often he'd asked questions about Mickey, how curious he'd been as to where Mickey might be, if he had contacted her. Why hadn't she seen his deception before the moment he'd identified himself? Why hadn't she realized the laid-back, sexy ranch foreman was asking far too many questions about a man who was an absent boss?

She'd been such a fool. She'd made it so easy for him. She'd just accepted him at face value, had clung to him in need and believed he was nothing more complicated than a cowboy who had lost his wife.

God, she didn't even know if that were true. He might have just made up the whole Rebecca thing in order to gain her sympathy.

She'd even called his last employee to check him out. The call had probably gone to another FBI agent who had pretended to be a rancher Rhett had once worked for. This entire thing had been a well-oiled operation and she and Esme had just been two women to exploit.

Why wasn't she crying? Her heart had never felt so battered, so broken, and yet it was as if the pain was too intense for the mere release of tears.

The front door opened and closed and she steeled herself as he walked back into the living room. "I don't want to hear anything you have to say," she said, vaguely surprised by the bitterness in her voice.

"Caitlin, please. Just hear me out. I know I've hurt you and that's the last thing I ever wanted to do. I had a job to do and I'm sorry that you had to be part of it." His voice was lower than usual, heavy with obvious regret.

She stared at him. "You lied to me about who you were and what you'd experienced in your life. Every move you've made while here was a calculated one to get close to me so you could get to my father."

"That's not true," he protested.

"Was it under orders that you took me to bed?"

His green eyes were dark, haunted as he held her gaze. "Of course not, and I didn't lie to you about my life, Caitlin. My parents really were rodeo people who died in a car wreck. I was a rancher. I lost my wife in a riding accident and sold the ranch and for the next six months reeled in grief. I wound up in Detroit and joined the police force, made detective in record time and was recruited by the FBI when I found out some information about the Raven's Head Society. That society puts our national security at risk and we knew that your father had information we needed." The words spilled out of him as if forced by enormous pressure.

"Fine," she snapped. "You got what you wanted. There's no reason for you to hang around any longer. Wait." She lifted a hand to her ear. "I think I hear that crazy wind blowing, and that means it's time for you to move along, cowboy."

He winced, as if finding her sarcasm physically painful. "I don't want to leave it like this between us, Caitlin. You need to know that it wasn't all about the job." He took a step toward the sofa but before he could get too close she jumped up and backed away from him.

She didn't want him close enough to her that she could smell his familiar scent, she didn't want to see the little gold flecks in his deep green eyes and remember how he'd gazed up at her as they'd made love.

"Please, just go," she said wearily. Couldn't he see that just by standing here in front of her he was breaking her heart yet again? She just wanted him gone. The numbness was starting to wear off and she was having difficulty reclaiming her anger. Instead, a deep grief was welling up inside her, a grief that had tears burning at her eyes once again. And the last thing she wanted was for him to see her weep.

"I don't want to go without letting you know that you got to me, that when I held you in my arms it wasn't just because I was told to do whatever necessary to get close to you, it was because I wanted you there. I need you to know that when I made love to you it was real and it had nothing to do with the reason I was here." He held out his hands in front of him, as if beseeching her to listen...to understand.

"So, what do you want? A medal for going above and beyond the call of duty?"

He dropped his hands to his sides. "No, I just want you to understand that I care about you, that this was hard on me, too. I had a job to do, but the last thing I wanted was to hurt you." His voice held a wealth of emotion, but it didn't touch her.

Suddenly her anger was back, bigger than ever. "I'm sorry this was all so tough on you, but I never lied to you about who I was. I never lied to you about how I felt. I trusted you." Her voice raised and she wondered how a heart could break over and over again.

She drew a deep, weary sigh. "At least the men in the jungle who hurt me didn't pretend to be anything other than what they were."

He looked as if she'd slapped him. His face paled and he took a step backward as if physically shoved by her words. "Then I guess there's nothing more that I can say to you except I'm sorry, Caitlin. I'm so damned sorry."

He didn't wait for her reply but instead turned on his heels and left. She held onto her control until she heard the door close behind him and only then did the tears that she'd fought so hard to hold back release in a torrent of utter heartbreak.

Sobbing in deep gasps, she climbed the stairs to her

room, just wanting to hide, to escape from the pain that Rhett Kane had left behind.

It was noon when Hank called his two sons into the great room to speak to them. He'd been doing a lot of thinking since his talk with President Joe Colton and then again after talking to Mickey O'Donahue early that morning.

Mickey had told him he was turning himself in to the authorities. He'd told Hank that his daughter had been raped and Mickey wasn't protecting any of the bastards in the society any longer. As he'd heard about Caitlin's rape a new horror had filled Hank's soul as he thought of his own daughter held by somebody in the society.

President Joe Colton had talked to Hank about the importance of family, and knowing the sacrifice Mickey was making to avenge Caitlin's rape had stirred a fierce, unexpected love of family in Hank.

He still hadn't heard from the kidnappers, but he knew it was only a matter of time before he did. And it was his love for his daughter that had driven him finally to make the decision he'd reached.

Hank knew he should be in FBI custody and the only reason he wasn't was that he was an active participant in Lana's kidnapping. Once Lana was home safe and sound Hank knew he'd be arrested and probably spend the rest of his life in prison, unless he could cut some sort of deal. But at the moment he wasn't interested in deals. He just wanted his daughter home.

"What's up?" Cole asked as he and Dylan came into the room.

The sight of his handsome twin sons brought a sudden lump to Hank's throat. They were both good men, successful men, no thanks to him. All of his sons were good men.

He'd been gone throughout most of their lives, wheeling and dealing in Washington, D.C., building his wealth and power at the expense of his family, at the expense of real relationships with his sons. He hadn't taken time with them, and now regrets filled Hank's soul.

"I've reached a decision and I wanted to speak to you about it," he began. "First of all, I want you to tell your brothers and your sister that I love them. I've loved you all, even though I know over the years I haven't shown it enough. And even though your mother isn't speaking to me and I don't even know where she is, please let her know that I'm sorry about everything, that I'll always love her, too."

Thick emotion suddenly pressed tight against Hank's chest. If he had it to do over again would he make the same mistakes? He liked to believe he wouldn't, but he wasn't so sure. The lure of power, of easy money and easy women had been so seductive, and ultimately he recognized that in many ways he was a weak man, but he didn't intend to be weak any longer.

"You said you'd reached a decision," Dylan said with a touch of impatience. "What decision?"

Hank straightened his shoulders and drew a deep

breath. "When the kidnappers contact me again I intend to offer myself in exchange for Lana."

"Dad, you can't do that," Cole protested, his eyes darkening. "They'll kill you."

"Probably," Hank agreed. "But I'll die knowing that Lana is safe, and that's all that's important."

"Are you sure about this?" Dylan asked.

"I've never been surer of anything in my life," Hank replied. "My life for hers." As Hank said the words he felt the rightness of it in his very soul. And if that wasn't enough, for the first time in years he saw the respect that lit his sons' eyes, and he realized that that was worth all the power, all the money in the world.

Chapter 12

"Good morning," Caitlin greeted Esme as Caitlin entered the kitchen.

"Good morning to you," Esme replied as Caitlin walked to the coffeemaker and poured herself a cup of coffee. With cup in hand, she went to the table and sat, smiling as Esme took a seat across from her. "You slept well?"

Caitlin shrugged. "Okay, I guess." It had been only two days since her father had been taken away, a little over forty-eight hours since Rhett had left, but a lot had happened in those two days.

Her father had called the day before to tell her that he was fine, being treated well and expected to be home soon. He'd been told that as long as he fully cooperated he wouldn't be looking at any jail time. And he was fully cooperating, telling everything he knew about the secret society.

He'd also told her that he'd heard the news from several FBI agents that Marc Jiminez was dead.

The official story was that there had been a war between two drug factions and Marc had been killed in a raid on his house. But Caitlin suspected that somebody had been dispatched to take out the man who had been part of the Raven's Head organization, a man who had nothing good to offer to society.

She'd also heard from Garrett Simms, who'd called from a rehab center and told her he'd finally decided to get help for his alcoholism.

"We'll both sleep better once your father is home again," Esme said, pulling Caitlin from her thoughts.

Caitlin nodded and took a sip of her coffee, but she knew it would take a long time before Rhett would stop haunting her dreams.

"Your father called early this morning," Esme continued. "He proposed to me again and this time I told him yes."

"Oh, Esme, I'm so happy for you, for Dad." Caitlin jumped out of her chair and gave the older woman a hug.

"I don't want a big wedding, just the three of us here at the ranch with a preacher," Esme said as Caitlin returned to her chair.

"We'll go shopping together for a beautiful lace wedding gown," Caitlin said. "And you'll be so gorgeous that day you'll take Dad's breath away."

Esme giggled like a teenager. "I'd like that," she agreed. "You'll be my maid of honor." She reached across the table and took Caitlin's hand in hers. "And you will always be the daughter I dreamed of having when I was young."

Caitlin's heart swelled with love for the woman who had taken on a widower and his young daughter and cared for them, loved them with all her heart.

For the next few minutes they talked about weddings. At least through all the bad that had happened, Mickey and Esme's relationship had come to light, a shining example of true, enduring love.

Caitlin had been foolish to entertain the hope that she might find that same kind of love with the cowboy who called himself Randall.

She willed away any thought of Rhett Kane. There was no point in thinking about him, no point in wishing things had been different.

After breakfast she left the house and walked out to the small corral. The midmorning sun warmed her shoulders as she sweet-talked Molly, who stood several feet away from her, refusing to come any closer.

During the past two days Caitlin had tried to stay as busy as possible. She'd cleaned out her closet and prepared a box of clothing for charity. She'd spent some time with the newspaper checking out rental space to open her own office, and she'd tried desperately not to think about Rhett Kane.

But her thoughts kept returning to the man who had become her bodyguard, her healer and her lover. The anger that had raged through her when she'd discovered his duplicity had given way to a yawning sadness.

There was a part of her that wanted to believe, that needed to believe that some of what they had shared had been real, had been true. Surely he wasn't so good at his job that he could manufacture the desire she'd seen shining in his eyes, the desire she'd tasted on his lips. Surely he wasn't such a good actor that it had all just been a game of pretend?

Not that it mattered. He'd told her that he hadn't lied about his life experiences. He had lost his wife and she had believed him when he'd told her he never wanted to get involved that deeply with anyone again. At least he'd been honest about that.

She released a deep sigh. He'd gone back to wherever he'd come from to get on with his life and she was determined to get on with hers. She'd made a list of things she wanted to accomplish in the next week or so. Cleaning the closet had been first on the list, but she also wanted to start the process of opening her own practice and find a therapist to work with just to make sure she was truly healing from the trauma she'd experienced.

She was strong, a survivor. She'd endured the rape and the attempts on her life. She'd lived through the worry about her father and the betrayal of Rhett Kane. She felt as if she could survive anything else life decided to throw her way.

"We made it, girl," she said softly to Molly. "We're both going to be just fine. All we need is time." Molly neighed as if in agreement.

Even though Esme had said she wanted a simple ceremony, Caitlin would make sure Esme's wedding day was one to remember. She could at least enjoy shopping for a dress for her, enjoy Esme's and her father's happiness in finally being united in marriage.

And it was time, past time, for Caitlin to leave her father's house and find a place of her own. The husband and the children would have to wait, but there was nothing holding her back from getting her own ranch and starting her life for real. Her father would be fine with Esme beside him and she'd be fine alone.

At that moment Caitlin heard the sound of a car approaching. She turned to look and felt as if every part of her body froze at the sight of Rhett's familiar pickup pulling up.

What was he doing here? What could possibly bring him back here? Maybe he had some loose ends to tie up. She desperately wanted to see him again. She desperately didn't want ever to see him again.

She fought the impulse to reach up to tidy her hair and instead gripped the post of the corral with one hand to steady herself as he stopped the car and got out.

The sunlight kissed his shaggy blond hair and a habitual five-o'clock shadow dusted his jaw. She tried not to remember how those whiskers had felt rubbing erotically against her skin. He was clad in a pair of tight dark jeans and a short-sleeved, white button-up shirt.

He looked handsome and sexy and she hated him just a little bit for making her want him all over again despite what had gone down between them.

He walked toward her and stopped when he was about three feet from her. "Hi."

"Hi," she replied, pleased that her voice held none of the inner turmoil the sight of him had stirred inside her.

"It's a beautiful day," he said. He sounded tentative, as if testing whether he'd be welcome or not.

How she wished she could reclaim her anger where he was concerned. Surely anger wouldn't hurt like the pain that sliced through her now.

"Yes, it's a nice day," she agreed. A nice day for another bout of heartache, she thought.

He shoved his hands in his pockets. "Have you heard from your father?"

She nodded, the movement feeling wooden. "He's doing okay and hopes to be home soon. He's been offered protective custody, but he's intent on coming back here and determined that he can take on any of the Raven's Head Society members that might still want to harm him."

"Good. I'm sure you and Esme are both eager to get him back home."

"He called this morning and asked Esme to marry him. She agreed, so it looks like there will be a wedding on the ranch sometime after he gets home."

"That's great news, right?" He pulled his hands out of his pockets and took a step closer to her.

"It's wonderful news." She tightened her grip on the fence post to keep herself firmly in place. She wanted to run away from him. She desperately wanted to run into his arms.

"What are you doing here?" she asked.

He frowned. "I don't know where else to go."

She looked at him curiously. "All the bad guys in the world have been caught and put behind bars so you don't have another assignment to go to?"

"I took a leave of absence." He took another step toward her. "For the first time in years I'm seeing things more clearly and I realized I needed to make some decisions about what I want to do with the rest of my life, and being an FBI agent isn't top of my list."

She told herself she didn't want to know what he intended to do with the rest of his life. She didn't want to have any information that would make her wonder about him, worry about him at any time in the future.

"But what about the Raven's Head Society and the threat against President Colton?" she asked.

"There are plenty of other men working to keep the president safe and get the bad guys behind bars," he replied. "They don't need me."

He stepped up next to her and grabbed the top of the fence railing with one hand. This close she could see the tired lines that radiated from his eyes. He looked like a man who had found sleep difficult for the past couple of nights. That definitely made two of them.

"The last couple of days I've been thinking a lot about Rebecca." His gaze shot out to the distant pasture. "In the past when I thought about her I focused on the moment of her death, got stuck in that terrible moment in time. But this time I started thinking about how happy I'd been with her."

What was he doing to her? Caitlin watched as his features softened, as his eyes took on the hazy quality of memories. Why was he telling her how much he'd loved his wife? Why was he twisting the knife just a little deeper into her heart?

"I loved waking up with her so warm and soft in my arms. I loved the sound of her laughter and the way she made me feel as a man. And, in remembering all those good times, all the happiness I felt at that time in my life, I realized that if I didn't love again that deeply, it's true that I'd never feel the pain of loss, but I would also be depriving myself of any hope of true happiness."

He turned and looked at her and in his eyes she saw a glimmer of something breathtaking, of something that both scared her and thrilled her. His eyes were filled with desire but also with something softer that made her heart hitch in her chest.

"Caitlin, I know I hurt you badly and I wish I could tell you that if I had it to do all over again, I'd do things differently, but I can't tell you that. I'd do it all again if I thought it might save the life of the president."

She nodded, appreciating his honesty and under-standing the high stakes that had been involved in this particular assignment. He'd had a duty to perform, an important duty that pertained to national security. How could she fault him for what he'd done?

"You still haven't answered my question of why you're here," she said.

"I'm here because I love waking up with you so soft and warm in my arms, Caitlin. I love the sound of your laughter and the way you make me feel when you look at me. I'm here because I don't want to be an FBI agent anymore. I want to do what I love, I want to ranch and I want you to be there with me. I want you riding next to me, building dreams with me. I want the picket fence and the children with you."

Her hand began to tremble on the post. She was so afraid to believe him, afraid that somehow this was all just another assignment and he was here to rip away another part of her heart.

"I have terrible nightmares," she blurted.

He smiled, his charming dimples flashing in his cheeks. "I know, and I want to be there every night for the rest of your life to hold you when you're scared, to comfort you when you cry."

"I'm going into therapy." She needed him to know what he was getting into, she needed to know that he could love her despite all her flaws.

"I think that's a great idea. I'll drive you to your appointments. I'll even go in with you and talk to the therapist if you need me to." His gaze remained steady on her. "I'm in it for the long haul, Caitlin. I want to build a life with you, to have children and grow old with you. I love you, Caitlin, I love you with all my heart and soul."

"What about the wind you told me about? The one that blows you from place to place?" she asked tentatively.

"As long as you're by my side I'll never hear that wind again."

Caitlin's heart soared with happiness. She believed him. She saw the love shining from his eyes, felt it radiating from him. "We do have a sudden opening for a foreman here," she said teasingly.

"I'll take it," he replied. "But just until we have a spread of our own. Are you going to kiss me now?" he asked.

"Yes, I believe I am." She finally let go of the post and stepped into his waiting embrace. Their lips met in a kiss that warmed Caitlin from her head to her toes, a kiss that spoke of love and desire and a commitment to last a lifetime.

As they broke the kiss Molly whinnied and walked toward where they stood outside the corral. She came close enough that Rhett stroked her nose. "I knew you were going to be okay," he said in obvious delight. Molly quickly stepped back, but the fact that she'd come close enough to Rhett to allow him to touch her spoke of the fact that she was truly going to be just fine.

And Caitlin knew she was going to be more than all right with a man who understood her, a man who supported her, a man whom she had a feeling would take her breath away for a long time to come.

Epilogue

Hank Kelley stood at the window in the bedroom and stared out unseeing at the pastures beyond. He rubbed a fist against his chest where a tight pressure inside felt as if it might blow at any minute. Although he'd always been the picture of good health, the stress was definitely getting to him.

Several times over the past couple of days he'd feared he might be having a heart attack, but he had ultimately recognized it was just the enormous stress that had been with him since he'd made the decision to change places with Lana.

He hadn't changed his mind about the decision. He was determined to do anything in his power to save his daughter's life.

He knew that once he took Lana's place with the

kidnappers he'd be dead within hours. Despite the fact that he was a man who had always loved life, a man who had been determined to squeeze every ounce of pleasure out of his time on earth, he didn't regret dying for his daughter.

Somebody else would have to bring down the Raven's Head Society, somebody else would have to see to it that President Colton remained safe. Hank's sole focus was his daughter's life.

Unfortunately, since he'd made his decision he still hadn't heard from the kidnappers and the silence was absolutely killing him. Why hadn't they contacted him? Why hadn't they provided the proof of life he'd demanded from them?

He'd finally made the right decision. He'd finally gotten the courage to sacrifice himself for his love of his daughter. His biggest fear at the moment was that it was too late, that Lana was already dead.

* * * * *

So you think you can write?

It's your turn!

Mills & Boon® and Harlequin® have joined forces in a global search for new authors and now it's time for YOU to vote on the best stories.

It is our biggest contest ever—the prize is to be published by the world's leader in romance fiction.

And the most important judge of what makes a great new story?

YOU—our reader.

Read first chapters and story synopses for all our entries at **www.soyouthinkyoucanwrite.com**

Vote now at www.soyouthinkyoucanwrite.com!

HARLEQUIN®
entertain, enrich, inspire™

MILLS & BOON®

A sneaky peek at next month...

INTRIGUE...

BREATHTAKING ROMANTIC SUSPENSE

My wish list for next month's titles...

In stores from 19th October 2012:

☐ High Noon – Debra Webb

& The Cop's Missing Child – Karen Whiddon

☐ The Reunion Mission – Beth Cornelison

& Kansas City Cowboy – Julie Miller

☐ Detective Daddy – Mallory Kane

& Engaged with the Boss – Elle James

☐ Missing Mother-To-Be – Elle Kennedy

In stores from 2nd November 2012:

☐ Savour the Danger – Lori Foster

Available at WHSmith, Tesco, Asda, Eason, Amazon and Apple

Just can't wait?

1012/46